BHRODI'S ANGEL

De Wolfe Pack
The Series

Meara Platt

DE WOLFE PACK: THE SERIES

By Alexa Aston
Rise of de Wolfe

By Amanda Mariel
Love's Legacy

By Anna Markland
Hungry Like de Wolfe

By Autumn Sands
Reflection of Love

By Barbara Devlin
Lone Wolfe: Heirs of Titus De Wolfe Book 1
The Big Bad De Wolfe: Heirs of Titus De Wolfe Book 2
Tall, Dark & De Wolfe: Heirs of Titus De Wolfe Book 3

By Cathy MacRae
The Saint

By Christy English
Dragon Fire

By Hildie McQueen
The Duke's Fiery Bride

By Kathryn Le Veque
River's End

By Lana Williams
Trusting the Wolfe

By Laura Landon
A Voice on the Wind

By Leigh Lee
Of Dreams and Desire

By Mairi Norris
Brabanter's Rose

By Marlee Meyers
The Fall of the Black Wolf

By Mary Lancaster
Vienna Wolfe

By Meara Platt
Nobody's Angel
Bhrodi's Angel
Kiss an Angel

By Mia Pride
The Lone Wolf's Lass

By Ruth Kaufman
My Enemy, My Love

By Sarah Hegger
Bad Wolfe on the Rise

By Scarlett Cole
Together Again

By Victoria Vane
Breton Wolfe Book 1
Ivar the Red Book 2
The Bastard of Brittany Book 3

By Violetta Rand
Never Cry de Wolfe

TABLE OF CONTENTS

CHAPTER ONE

Pembroke, Wales
September 1816

"MISS PERTWEE, GET off those rocks. I've warned you before." Bhrodi de Shera, the tenth Duke of Pembroke, left the hillside walking trail that hugged the coastal cliffs of Pembroke and strode toward Prudence Pertwee with a frown that she could not possibly ignore, but she managed to do so anyway. *Irritating girl.*

"Good morning, Your Grace." Prudence lowered her spyglass and smiled brightly at him. She brushed back a lock of her fiery red hair that had blown onto her forehead and calmly waited for him to climb the few rocks to reach her side. "Have you come to join us?"

"No, Miss Pertwee. I want you off this ledge." He repeated his command, wondering how a young woman who barely came up to his shoulder could have so much obstinance packed into her slender body. Her companions looked suitably frightened of him. Why couldn't she respond the same way? It was barely after sunrise and the autumn sun was only now burning away the mist that hovered over the windswept sea and clung to the slippery rocks below. "You'll hurt yourself."

"I haven't yet. I understand the danger and am always careful. Especially up here." She was standing on an exposed outcropping at the edge of Bhrodi's property, a high promontory that jutted out over the now glistening white-capped sea. The wind was quite fierce up here, blowing her serviceable gown of forest green wool flat against her shapely body, but she appeared as determined to ignore its strong gusts as she was to ignore him.

"I'll give you to the count of three."

She brushed back another loose strand that had escaped her neat bun because of the steady wind and cast him a defiant look.

"One... two..."

"But the black-tailed godwits have started their migration," she said with an exasperated huff. "So have the cormorants and gannets. Your cliffs are filled with them. Do stay and watch them with us. We'd love to have your company." She forced an annoyingly effervescent smile that rankled him. *She* rankled him. Especially because he knew that she didn't mean a word of her invitation. She thought he was an ogre. She'd called him that before.

He sighed.

She was still smiling at him in a soft, beautiful way that almost had him believing she was sincere.

No one should be permitted to look so lovely – or cheerful, for that matter – before the breakfast hour. It was only a short while after sunrise and here she was, chirping away as happily as those birds she was so diligently watching.

"I don't care if their tails are black or yellow or purple." Bhrodi deepened his frown at the young woman who had been leading the Pembroke chapter of the Ladies Birdwatching Society across his cow pasture toward Llangolyn Rock to observe said black-tailed godwits every day for the past three weeks. "You are trespassing on my property and I want you off it now."

The sun chose just that moment to shine upon her glorious red curls, seeming to turn them to silken flame. The impertinent Miss Pertwee also had green eyes the exotic color of jade that were quite exquisite, even as she insolently glowered at him. "We've had this conversation before, Your Grace. Every day for the past three weeks, to be precise. My answer to you is still the same. Your father, the late Duke of Pembroke, granted our society the unfettered right to cross your lands. Your cliffs are a feeding ground for goshawks and choughs and your particular favorite," she said, her voice laced with sarcasm, "the black-tailed godwit."

"Don't forget to mention your great tits, Miss Pertwee," intoned a bombazine clad matron with an insufferable air of authority.

Bhrodi's heart stopped.

Indeed, Miss Pertwee had a great pair of... blast, he was in for it now. The girl knew exactly what he was thinking since his gaze had immediately shot to her breathtakingly perfect bosom at the comment. He'd only looked for an instant before hastily turning away, but she'd noticed. Nothing ever escaped her sharp gaze and that irritated him as well.

He groaned and ran a hand roughly through his hair. No, he wasn't going to say it. But yes, she had the most magnificent pair of... and what idiot had come up with such a name for a bird? A tit. Seriously? And its cousin, the great tit.

How could one speak of that bird without sounding lewd?

And how could one look at Miss Pertwee without noticing…

Her beautiful eyes narrowed in warning.

Bhrodi turned away from her to wave everyone off the outcropping. Since he was the present Duke of Pembroke, they all immediately obeyed. All but the stubborn Miss Pertwee. He turned back to her with a grunt. "The wind is quite strong today. I'd hate for you to lose your footing and fall. It's dangerous out here." For more reasons than a treacherous cliff face.

The wind chose just that moment to intensify to a gale force gust. It was as though some divine force had been listening to his words and thought to have a bit of perverse fun. Miss Pertwee staggered back and lost her balance when her foot struck a loose rock that rolled out from under her.

Bhrodi reached out to grab her by one of her flailing arms.

He tried to be gentle, but it was either pull her hard toward him or allow her to fall. So he pulled and she slammed with an *oof* against his chest, her soft body

5

molding to his in that instant and shocking both of them with the unexpected heat of that impact. He wrapped his arms around her. She slid her hands up his chest to grab onto his shoulders and cling to them with all her might.

One… two… three… four… five seconds passed.

Her eyes widened in sudden awareness.

She gave a cry and pushed off him with all haste.

In the next moment, she cried out again, but this time in pain. She'd twisted her ankle on that loose rock. Her leg buckled out from under her when she made the mistake of putting her weight on it. She fell to the ground before Bhrodi could catch her. "Blessed saints, are you all right?"

"Miss Pertwee!" The members of her society flocked around her like the birds they were studying. "You're hurt. Can you walk?"

"Yes, I'm sure I can." But her eyes were glistening with threatened tears that indicated otherwise. She attempted to rise and sank back with another soft cry.

Bhrodi ordered everyone to stand back while he knelt beside her and untied her boot lace. "Your foot will swell. Did you feel a bone break?"

She shook her head. "No, I think I've just sprained

my ankle. Of all the wretched luck."

He took hold of her leg, ignoring the jolt of heat that shot through him at the mere touch of the girl, and very gently tugged off her boot. He wasn't attracted to this impertinent nuisance. Not in the least. That his blood was on fire had nothing to do with her or the divine softness of her body. "You're fortunate you didn't tumble off the cliff ledge," he muttered angrily, although he was angrier with himself for liking everything about this girl.

His unexpected response to her nearness was not her fault, but he blamed her anyway.

"I suppose I ought to be grateful to you." She sighed and eased back. "Indeed, I am. Truly. You saved my life. Thank you, Your Grace."

He grumbled an acceptance. "You're obviously incapable of walking. Here, put your arms around my neck." He ignored the excited whispers coming from Miss Pertwee's companions who were standing behind him.

Bollocks, what were these old hens going on about? The girl was injured. He wasn't romantically sweeping her off her feet.

He turned to the ladies, instantly stopping their

chatter. "Today's excursion is at an end. Return to town, but make certain to stay on the walking paths and don't stray off them. I'll deliver Miss Pertwee home in my carriage."

"She ought to have a chaperone," the bombastic lady who'd spoken earlier intoned.

Indeed, she ought to, but he wasn't about to invite the entire society into his home. It was his sanctuary. His private retreat. If he'd wanted company, he'd be in London enjoying the amusements offered by the sophisticated women who populated the *demi-monde*. "Do you doubt my honor?"

He'd been raised to be a duke and knew how to cut a person down to size with one frosty stare. The woman immediately backed down. "No, Your Grace. Your reputation is impeccable."

Even if it wasn't – which it certainly wasn't – no one would ever dare tell him so to his face.

He helped Miss Pertwee to her feet.

She took great care to put her weight only on her uninjured leg. "I think I can manage if I lean against someone sturdy and then hop."

"Don't be ridiculous." He scooped her into his arms. She wasn't heavy. Indeed, she had a slender

8

build. Trim waist, narrow hips. Light bones.

But she was soft and full up front where it counted.

He might find her irresistible if she weren't so irritating.

"Wait!" she cried as he was about to carry her off. "I mustn't forget my spyglass. It's over there, by the loose rock."

One of her younger female companions picked it up and handed it to her. "Oh, Prudence. I hope the glass isn't broken."

Miss Pertwee smiled kindly at the young woman whose blonde curls were neatly fashioned atop her head and who had pleasant, bright blue eyes. She appeared to be an amiable, biddable sort of girl. One who respected rank and stature, unlike the young woman in his arms who challenged him at every turn. "I'm sure it's fine. Thank you, Lucinda. It fell onto the grass, not against the rocks."

Bhrodi cleared his throat to put an end to their conversation. He wanted Prudence Pertwee out of his arms and away from him as quickly as possible. "I'll have my estate manager put up warning signs around this outcropping. If I catch any of you here again, I'll toss you off the cliffs myself."

He got the desired response, a collective gasp from the ladies, except from Miss Pertwee who called him a cobble-headed dunce. She'd muttered it under her breath, but she was in his arms and her lips were close to his ear, so of course he'd heard the insult.

He chose to overlook it.

Prudence was getting under his skin in too many ways this morning. Besides, he had more important matters to worry about than her or her squawking birds. Falling rocks, for one. Smugglers, for another. There were caves used by them all along the coastline. What if Prudence accidentally spotted smugglers hiding their wares in one of those caves? What if she decided to investigate on her own?

Bhrodi had been investigating a particularly nasty crew for the past two months, one that had caught the attention of those in the highest ranks of the royal circle. Prinny himself had asked Bhrodi to return to Pembroke to discover the identity of their leader. No one knew who this man was, only that he went by the name of Mongoose.

It was a purposeful insult to Bhrodi. Indeed, a brash challenge, for everyone knew that Bhrodi was a direct descendant of the legendary Serpent, one of the bravest warriors ever to fight for Wales.

A mongoose killed snakes and this man had twice attempted to kill him. This was a direct challenge. For this reason, Bhrodi had immediately accepted to act as an agent for the Crown.

It was a matter of family honor.

Bhrodi even bore the Serpent's name, Bhrodi de Shera. How could he not step in and destroy those who dishonored his family?

But first, he had to get rid of this irritating beauty in his arms.

She was too distracting.

He needed to concentrate on breaking up the ring of smugglers.

And stop thinking about how to get the luscious Miss Pertwee out of her clothes and into his bed.

CHAPTER TWO

P RUDENCE HAD NEVER in her wildest dreams expected to be in a duke's arms. Especially not this forbidding duke. He never smiled. He wore a perpetual frown. Despite that, he was still the handsomest man ever to walk the rich, green hills of Wales.

He was big and powerful, almost mythical in aspect.

Hot buttered biscuits. The man's body is as hard as those rock cliffs he's always going on about.

She could feel the tug and flex of his solid muscles as he effortlessly carried her back to his magnificent manor house. He was quite magnificent, as well. There was something in the silvery gray of his eyes that struck her as eternal. He seemed to belong here, to be as much a part of the tapestry of Wales as the beautiful mountains of Snowdonia or these rugged cliffs along the coastline that were hewn from nature's anger and the constantly pounding ocean waves.

Although his hair was black and eyes were a piercing silver-gray, he had a grace and strength similar to that of the red dragon of Wales. Of course, his bloodline was that of the Serpent, but was that mythical creature so different from a dark and fiery dragon?

"Why are you staring at me, Miss Pertwee?" the duke asked as he carried her across his sheep meadow, his determined strides never once breaking with fatigue. His home was now in view, it's imposing stone towers soaring above the treetops.

"Your face intrigues me, Your Grace. I know your ancestor was the Serpent, but you don't strike me as the slithery sort." Nor did he smell like a creature who slid along the ground. His was a divine scent of sandalwood and rugged sea air.

"Not the slithery sort?" He surprised her with a rich, deep laugh. "Should I take that as a compliment?"

She felt the heat of a blush creep into her cheeks. "Yes, I think you should. Forgive me, Your Grace. I speak my mind a little too often. But I did mean it in the best way. A serpent is known to move fast and strike with lethal impact. However, it is not a majestic creature like a dragon or a lion. And you are quite majestic."

He glanced at her with the trace of a smile on his nicely formed lips. "Another compliment?"

She nodded. "Perhaps it is because you have a little of the wolf in you as well. It is common knowledge that the Serpent took William de Wolfe's youngest daughter as his wife. So I think that in you, the mix of wolf and serpent makes for a remarkable blend."

"What about you, Miss Pertwee? How would you describe yourself?"

She shrugged her shoulders. "If I must, then I'd probably say that I am a very ordinary chough," she said, pronouncing it as *chuff*, which was its proper pronunciation. "It's a noisy bird sometimes referred to as a red-legged crow. Nothing as grand as a falcon or hawk or your dragon. Like the chough, I chatter too much. Most men find my opinions offensive to their ears. Choughs are not migratory creatures. They stay in one place, as I have for all of my life. They are also very loyal to their mates. I would be, if I ever married. But that isn't likely to happen. I've never felt… never mind. I have no experience in such matters. I'm not likely to, either."

She was almost one and twenty. Her birthday was

next month. Not that there was much to celebrate. Her father had remarried last year and her new stepmother had taken charge of the household. Eleanora was a nice woman, a very maternal sort who constantly fussed over her and her father. Her father adored being treated like a pampered child.

Prudence did not take to it nearly as well. She'd been in charge of the Pertwee household ever since her mother's death eight years ago and had done a good job of running it even at her young age. But two efficient women could not be in charge of one home. Prudence was not needed. This was no longer *her* roost to rule.

However, there was nowhere for her to go unless she married.

Unfortunately, no man had come close to proposing.

She was fully to blame, of course. It was all her fault. She'd put off every man who'd ever come around to call on her. She had to stop doing that, she supposed.

She studied the duke's handsome face. He was a wealthy man, and that alone would have been enough to tempt most women. But he was also spectacular looking, so every woman from nine to ninety had to be after him.

He'd resisted so far. Why hadn't he married? Any woman would have accepted him. It was time. He was almost thirty years old, or so she'd heard. Was he holding out for love?

"You're still staring at me, Miss Pertwee."

She nibbled her lip in consternation, for she really wanted to ask him why he was still a bachelor. Not that she had a proprietary interest in him. No, indeed. He was so far above her station that she'd have to tip her head back just to look up at his toes. "I wish to ask you some questions."

He arched a dark eyebrow. "What sort of questions?"

She winced. "Personal ones."

To her surprise, he shook his head and laughed. "Go ahead, ask them. However, I can't promise to answer them."

"Fair enough." She nodded. In truth, it was more than fair of him and that surprised her. She'd never considered that this frosty duke might be nice under all those layers of thick ice. "You haven't taken a wife yet."

"Is that a question?"

She sighed. "Why haven't you taken a wife?"

"None of your business."

"I know it is none of my business, but you said I could ask and I did warn you that my questions were personal. Are you holding out for love?" She hoped that she hadn't sounded too starry-eyed and breathless. She was merely asking out of curiosity, not out of any design for herself. "I hope you do."

His brow was still arched in that handsomely dangerous way, but his expression seemed to soften. "That is also none of your business, Miss Pertwee."

"I know. But I hope you do hold out for it. I think you would be a man much improved by love."

He gave a short bark of laughter. "I think you've just insulted me."

"I didn't mean to. You are surly and abrupt, surely you know that. And there's something quite forbidding in your aspect. Most people are afraid of you. It has nothing to do with your wealth or title. I think they'd be afraid of you even if you were a scholar or a fisherman. You have an air of danger about you. An aura of lethal power, just like your ancestor, the Serpent."

"What about you, Miss Pertwee. Will you hold out

for love?"

"Unfortunately, yes. I'm a common chough, don't forget. When I mate, it must be for life. I never stray far from my nest. However, I must find a new nest rather soon. My father's new wife has taken over ours and I am only in the way. She has every right to it, of course. She and my father are very happy." She shook her head and sighed. "I don't know how to go about falling in love. And who would love a common chough?"

He set her down on the front steps of his home and stared down at her. "There is nothing common about you, Prudence. Don't let anyone tell you otherwise."

His butler must have noticed their approach and opened the door just then. "Your Grace, is the young lady hurt?"

The duke nodded. "Yes, Bigbury. But not too badly. Summon Colliers. Have him bring my carriage around."

"At once, Your Grace." His butler hurried off to call for his coachman, leaving them alone once more.

The duke planted his booted foot beside her on the step and leaned forward to speak to her. "Are you thirsty? Too warm outdoors? I can carry you inside if you prefer."

Her eyes widened in surprise. "You would admit me into your home?"

"You mean my serpent's lair?" His grin was surprisingly appealing. She thought he didn't like her. So why was he being unexpectedly polite? Perhaps she'd misjudged him. "I would admit you in only as far as my drawing room. And reluctantly so. I wouldn't invite you in at all if you weren't hurt. You are far too snoopy for my comfort."

She shook her head and laughed. "Now that's the duke I've come to know and dislike. Although I must admit, I don't dislike you nearly as much as I thought I would."

"Was that a compliment or an insult?"

"A little of both, I think." She cast him an apologetic smile. "Have you had your fill of me yet? May I ask more questions? Because one thing puzzles me greatly."

"And what is that?"

"Why are you so overset about our bird watching? It is harmless fun and also serves a useful purpose. We're very careful not to damage your property." She noticed him stiffen and realized she must have touched upon a sensitive matter. But why was he suddenly so tense?

He refused to answer.

Although he'd allowed her to ask her questions, he hadn't responded to a single one.

"Ah, here comes Colliers with the carriage." He opened the door once the carriage had rolled to a stop in front of them, and then carefully lifted her onto the soft, black leather seat.

It truly was the finest carriage she'd ever seen. She admired everything about it, including the ducal crest, a black serpent upon a field of gold, that was emblazoned on the shining black door. The serpent's body was coiled and its head was upraised, as though about to strike with lethal force.

The duke climbed in after her and settled his large frame on the seat opposite hers. She could envision this man as a battle-hardened, medieval warrior. Despite his rank and fashionable upbringing, there was nothing soft about this Duke of Pembroke.

If he or his loved ones were ever threatened, this man would go in for the kill.

"Your Grace–"

"No more questions, Miss Pertwee."

"Very well, but won't you please call me Prudence?

You called me that a few moments ago and I rather liked it. I don't wish us to be enemies. I know we shall never be dear friends, but we can be friendly acquaintances, can't we?"

He cast her an intense look that suggested they would never be friends or even friendly acquaintances. But it wasn't an angry look that one would give an enemy. It was a hot look, perhaps smoldering. And now he appeared irritated. She sighed. She couldn't make out what that look meant.

"You'd better keep off that foot for several days," he muttered. "I would recommend at least a week to give the sprain time to mend."

He was right, but a week under the same roof as Eleanora Crompton Pertwee, her overly protective stepmother, would be insufferable. Eleanora would be in her glory, fluffing up Prudence's pillows, feeding her porridge as though she were an infant and incapable of feeding herself, constantly fussing and fretting over her. And there would be no escape. She couldn't run off on an injured foot.

Anyway, where would she go?

Eleanora wasn't to blame. It wasn't her fault that she exuded warmth and hospitality. She would have been a good mother to her children, only she'd never had any. She and her first husband, Thomas Crompton, were never blessed with any. She was too old now to bear children, so all those maternal efforts were trained on Prudence.

"Are you listening to me, Miss Pertwee?"

"Yes, I've heard your every word."

He cast her a wry grin, a most appealing grin that caused her heart to flutter. "I wasn't certain. Sometimes I think your birds pay me more heed than you do."

Prudence knew she was far too independent. It was a quality frowned upon in a wife. But she longed to do something important, to be someone important and admired by others just as her own mother had been.

Since university was out of the question for females, she'd studied on her own and taken it upon herself to research birds of the area in the hope of turning her findings into a book someday. She hoped it would be of merit to the birdwatching community. In any event, she enjoyed getting up early to study the varieties that nested among the nearby cliffs.

She would often lose herself for hours in her explorations, returning home shortly before sundown because it wasn't safe to walk those cliffs at night. The routine suited her and Eleanora very well.

But she was hobbled now and couldn't move around. Perhaps her friend, Lucinda, would come over and they could spend these next few days sequestered in her father's library to work on that book. They were neighbors and had been the very best of friends ever since they were infants in leading strings.

She would have done the same for Lucinda if ever the need arose.

The duke cleared his throat to regain her attention. "We've arrived, Miss Pertwee. Let me help you into your home."

She wanted to refuse the duke's offer, but couldn't. Her ankle was badly swollen and hurt like blazes. She needed to wrap it in a cold cloth and elevate it. However, first she had to climb the few stairs into her house. She couldn't manage even that without his assistance.

The duke lifted her into his divinely muscled arms and carried her inside. "Where shall I deposit you?"

Ah, the man was charming.

He made her feel like a milk bottle that needed to be set aside somewhere so that its contents wouldn't curdle. "Our parlor will be fine. One of the maids will help me upstairs."

She'd never been inside his home, but she knew that even if the walls were crumbling down around his broad shoulders, his home would still be grander than hers. Her father was the local magistrate, and although he held a respectable position, his income was not nearly as respectable. They lived comfortably, but very simply.

Had her father been a less honest man, they would have been wealthy. He was constantly offered bribes that he turned down. Prudence was proud of him.

"Ah, there's Molly," she said as the Pertwee's elderly housemaid lumbered by a few moments after the duke had set her down on the divan. Prudence called out to her. "I need a little help on the stairs, Molly. Will you be so kind as to assist me?"

"Of course, Miss Prudence."

But the duke stopped Molly as she was about to do so. "I'll carry her up to her bedchamber. Lead the way."

Although it was scandalous for him to suggest such a thing, he went up a notch in Prudence's estimation. Molly was old and frail, barely able to manage the stairs on her own, much less help Prudence climb up them. In all likelihood, they would have both taken a bad tumble, landing in a messy heap at the duke's feet.

Eleanora bustled in before the duke had the chance to lift her back into his arms. "Your Grace! This is an honor. To what do we owe…" She noticed Prudence's swollen foot. "Oh, dear. What happened to the poor child?"

Child?

When she was almost on the verge of becoming an old maid?

"She slipped on a rock while trespassing on my property."

Eleanora gave a nervous, twittering laugh. "Ah, bird watching again. She won't be scampering up there any more. I'll see to it, Your Grace. You won't be bothered any longer by Prudence. No, indeed. May I offer you refreshments?"

The duke shook his head. "No. I'll leave her to your capable care. She'll need help up the stairs. Good day, ladies."

Eleanora began to fuss over her the moment the duke was out the door. "Oh, Pru! You were up there again? The duke warned you to stay away, but do you ever listen to anyone? You might have been killed."

"But I wasn't. I merely twisted my ankle, and I

wouldn't have done that if he hadn't distracted me with his idiotic demands."

"I shall have to tell your father about this. He's probably heard it already from the local gossips. How will you ever catch a husband if your heart is always with those birds? And what of the duke?"

Prudence gazed at her in confusion. "What about him?"

"He did not look at all pleased. I suppose you insulted him."

Heat rose in Prudence's cheeks. "I suppose I did. But I didn't mean to. He's just so arrogant and full of himself. Just because he's a duke doesn't mean he knows anything about anything. He certainly doesn't know a thing about birds or understand how important they are to the balance of nature."

Eleanora sighed. "He doesn't have to. He's a handsome and wealthy duke."

Prudence rolled her eyes. "There's that blighted word again. *Duke.* Any dullard can be a duke, it's just a matter of parentage and luck of one's birth order. He isn't a divine being who descended from the heavens on a magnificent, golden chariot. He doesn't belch pearls. No celestial light emanates around him whenever he speaks. He leaves no trail of rose petals wherever he walks. The man is rude. He's always scowling at me. He… oh, dear. He's back."

"What?" Eleanora turned to follow her gaze.

The duke stepped through the parlor doorway, dominating the room as he stood before them in all his powerful glory. His gaze was lethally calm. His quiet fury scared the wits out of Prudence, but she refused to show it.

Her stepmother was noticeably trembling. "I think I need my smelling salts," she said, obviously wishing to flee the room, but the duke looked angry enough to snort flames as he stood with his arms folded across his chest, blocking the doorway. Eleanora looked like she wanted to dig a big hole in the parlor and hide herself in it.

"Miss Pertwee, do you always speak so disrespectfully of others when their backs are turned?" His frown deepened and he flexed his shoulders, which made him appear as big and breathtakingly muscular as a fierce medieval warrior. She'd seen a portrait of his ancestor, the Serpent. The current duke looked twice as daunting.

"Never. I am always polite except with you. You're

the only one who's given me cause."

Eleanora gasped. "Prudence!"

"Well, he has Eleanora." Prudence returned his steady gaze. How much had he heard? Everything? Drat, she would have curbed her tongue had she noticed him standing there. He ought to have climbed in his carriage and been well on his way to Pembroke Hall by now. What was he doing back here? Oh, well. He hated her for life now, so it didn't much matter what else she said to him. "Will you dare deny that you are always scowling at me? I would show you proper respect if you were ever respectful to me. But you're not."

Eleanora gasped again. "Prudence! Enough!"

"Kindly leave us, Mrs. Pertwee. I wish to have a private word with your stepdaughter."

Prudence curled her hands into fists to brace herself for the blistering set down she was about to receive from him. Perhaps she ought to go on the offensive instead. She wasn't the sort to cower in fear. Anyway, he was already livid. How much angrier could he get? "Why did you come back in, Your Grace? I thought you'd left."

"Obviously." He unfolded his arms and held out his

hand to show her the object held in his outstretched palm. Her spyglass. "I came to return this. You left it in my carriage."

The impertinence drained from her.

In truth, he'd been patient and attentive to her today. He'd saved her from a nasty fall off that outcropping and taken the time out of his busy schedule to bring her home in his best carriage, no less. She'd returned his generosity with a spate of insults. "Thank you." She groaned lightly as she reached out to take the offered spyglass. "Sincerely, thank you. You needn't berate me. No need. I feel very much ashamed for the way I've treated you today."

He arched an eyebrow. "Just today?"

"No. For the past three weeks as well. Do you mind if I remove my boot? You unlaced it earlier, but my foot has swollen to twice its size and is quite painful." It was the truth. She wasn't merely trying to gain his pity, although it couldn't hurt to gain a little sympathy for her plight.

"Let me do it." He surprised her by bending on one knee before her and very gently easing it off her foot. He set it aside and then took the seat beside her. "Perhaps I have been a little abrupt with you lately."

"A little?" She cast him a wincing smile and shook her head. "Sorry. I'm doing it again. Do you think we might reach a compromise about our use of your land? You see, my friend Lucinda and I are studying the local avian population for a greater scientific purpose. If a man came to you and asked for access to your promontory for his scholarly research purposes, you'd grant it to him. I'm only asking that you show me the same courtesy."

He leaned forward, the muscles of his arms tensing as he did so. "What makes you think I would show him any courtesy?"

His silvery gaze was upon her. She ought to have been quaking in her boots, but all she wanted to do was reach out and trace her fingers along the rugged contours of his face. What she really wanted to do was put her lips to his because she was achingly curious to kiss him. She did not understand why she felt this way, but there was no denying that he was handsome or that he made her body tingle.

It was the oddest sensation, but a nice one.

He was still looking at her, as though awaiting an answer. Goodness! His brooding eyes had a sensual, downward slant to them. Did all serpents have such sensual eyes? That explained why all the girls grew giddy around him. She was no exception, and that was most disappointing. She wished to be unique. Apparently, she wasn't. She swallowed hard. "Wouldn't you give more courtesy to a man?"

"No. I don't want anyone up there. It's too dangerous. The rocks are loose." He glanced at her swollen foot. "As you found out this morning."

She sighed. "Very well, we shall hunt for another location. But yours is the best. I'll–"

"You'll do no such thing," he interjected. "I don't want you anywhere near those cliffs or the surrounding beaches."

Her eyes narrowed as she returned his stare. "Now I'm not permitted anywhere near the coast? That's nonsensical. What is going on, Your Grace? This has nothing to do with me or my birds, has it?"

"Miss Pertwee, let me be clear about this. If I find you anywhere near those cliffs again, I shall have the magistrate lock you up."

She rolled her eyes. "You do know that the magistrate is my father, don't you?"

He groaned. "Must you always be so difficult?"

"I don't try to be. I think I am being quite reasonable. Let's try another approach, shall we? Instead of arguing over where I *cannot* go, let's agree upon where I *can* go on your property to watch the birds." She cast him a gracious smile that she hoped did not look forced.

He rose to his full, imposing height, once more folding his arms across his chest. He frowned down at her. "Nowhere, Miss Pertwee. If I catch you anywhere on my property again, I shall toss you into my dungeon. No magistrate, whatever his relation to you, will ever get you out."

"Pembroke Hall has a dungeon?"

His look was hot and intense and melted her bones instead of frightening her, as she knew he was trying to do. "I shall build one just for you."

"I suppose it shall have dank, slimy walls. Thick iron chains. Big, ugly rats to scamper at my feet." She ought to be scared, but smiled at him instead.

She knew she should be scared.

But the man had held her protectively in his arms for a solid ten minutes while carrying her back to his grand home. Ten minutes in his arms and her body had yet to recover from the shockingly pleasurable experience. She hadn't just been in his arms. She'd *felt* his every movement and the steady beat of his heart within his solid chest. She'd inhaled his divine, sandalwood scent. She'd cuddled against his big body, absorbing the masculine heat that radiated off him. The touch of his hands was like a hot caress upon her skin, even through her layers of clothing.

Then he'd seen her safely back to her own home.

While his heart had been beating slow and steady, hers hadn't stopped pounding all the while. Her bones had long ago turned soft as pudding. His every glance – even the glowering ones – now thrilled and delighted her.

This was a tragedy of epic proportions.

She was almost one and twenty, and had begun to despair of ever falling in love. But the oddest thing had happened to her while in his arms today.

She had fallen in love.

With *him*.

Sometimes life played cruel jests.

CHAPTER THREE

B HRODI'S BUTLER KNOCKED lightly at his open library door. Bhrodi looked up from his ledgers. "What is it, Bigbury?" He motioned for the man to step in and approach his large, ebony desk.

"A letter for you, Your Grace." He held out the crisp, ivory parchment.

Since Bigbury had earlier brought in the day's mail on a silver salver, Bhrodi knew that this note must have come by special messenger. He took it at once, certain it was important. Perhaps the results of the investigation on the first attempt on his life. But there was no seal on it. "Bollocks, it's another letter from *her*."

His butler's lips twitched as he tried to stave off a grin. "Yes, she delivered this one herself, but refused to stay. Her foot seems to have healed nicely. It's only been a week. I was certain it would take at least a fortnight for that nasty sprain to heal. But she's young and in good health. I suppose she'll be on those cliffs again tomorrow."

"Not if I have a say in the matter, which I do. Damn it, I'm the duke. She's supposed to obey me." But he knew that his title mattered not a whit to Prudence, the impertinent girl. "I ought to have built that dungeon," he muttered under his breath.

"Did you say dungeon, Your Grace?" Bigbury shook his head, certain he had misunderstood the mumbled words.

"Yes, I'm building one just for Miss Pertwee. Then I'm going to toss her in it if she dares defy me again." He ran a hand through his hair and sighed because they both knew it was nonsense. "What am I to do with her, Bigbury? We're so close to finding out the identity of the Mongoose. She's going to walk right into the trap we've laid for him and ruin everything."

"Since she seems unable to follow your simple orders, why not let her into your confidence and tell her about your plan? She could help. She's trustworthy and knows the terrain better than anyone in these parts. She's like an agile mountain goat, climbing up and down those cliffs without fear."

Bhrodi pushed out his chair and rose from behind his desk. "How do you know she's trustworthy? For all

I know, she could be working for the Mongoose."

"Your Grace!"

"Don't turn apoplectic, Bigbury. I know she isn't. She may be impertinent, but she's honest. Brutally honest, as I've had the misfortune to learn. She shows me no deference whatsoever." He found her frank opinions quite refreshing, but she was still a nuisance. "How long ago did she drop off that note?"

"Not long. I brought it straight in to you the moment she left."

He unfolded the parchment and read it aloud to Bigbury. The man was more than a butler. Both he and Colliers were former agents of the Crown, too old to remain in active service, but just the right age to provide wisdom and serve as background support for him.

Your Grace,

As I've dutifully sat with my foot upraised, slowly going insane with boredom, I am more certain than ever that something odd is going on with you. Not that you are odd. You're not. At least, not that I'm aware. You are merely surly. Is this why you have ignored my urgent letters regard-

ing my birds?

Bigbury burst out laughing. "Forgive me, Your Grace."

"You are most certainly not forgiven. Nor is she." However, Bhrodi could not help but laugh as well. "Blast, but she has a way of cutting me down to size. I'd never get too full of myself if she were... never mind. Perish the thought." He was going to say *if she were my wife*. That he would ever consider the possibility proved he had lost his sanity.

He resumed reading her letter.

My point is, something is going on in those cliffs that you do not want me or the Pembroke chapter of the Ladies Birdwatching Society to investigate. Smuggling, I assume. There are lots of caves within those cliffs that are suited to illegal activity. I know which ones are presently being used. There is one in particular that concerns me greatly. Would you care to know which one?

With impatient regards,
Prudence Pertwee

Since Bhrodi had been working in his shirt sleeves, he hastily donned his jacket and strode out after Prudence.

At least this note of hers made more sense than the other two she'd previously sent him. The first had merely said:

Romeo and Juliet are dead. This is most alarming. You must do something about it at once.

Respectfully,
Prudence Pertwee

The next note had been just as nonsensical:

I am bereft. Marc Anthony and Cleopatra are dead, too. When are you going to do something about it?

A little less respectfully,
Prudence Pertwee

It didn't take long for him to catch up to her. "Miss Pertwee, what are you going on about with these letters?"

She tipped her head in greeting, but she appeared more irritated with him than welcoming. Her chin shot up in defiance and her lips were pursed to convey her marked frustration. To his consternation, she simply looked irresistibly kissable to him. "Good afternoon, Your Grace. It's about time you paid attention to my plea for help."

A soft autumn breeze rustled her fiery hair causing a few wispy curls to blow onto her cheek. The sun shone down upon those glorious, silken strands, turning them to magnificent flame, and as she wrinkled her nose at him, he noticed several freckles on the bridge of her impudent nose. He frowned, something he always seemed to do around her. She had been right about that. But his frown was one of irritation with himself for suddenly wanting to kiss her with every ounce of his heart and soul.

Why was she affecting him this way? He didn't like this girl.

He'd gone after her merely because he was concerned for her. That was all. Nothing more.

She was injured, and yet she intended to climb those cliffs to find out what was happening to her birds. He couldn't allow her to put her life in danger. He'd have to take charge of the matter and deal quickly with their deaths. "Did you walk all the way to

Pembroke Hall on an injured foot? And don't give me that nonsense about being fine. It's obvious you are now in discomfort."

"Perhaps it hurts a little… maybe a lot." She sighed.

He resisted the urge to take her into his arms. The girl was strong willed. She'd manage on her own. She only needed to lean on the walking stick she had brought with her.

"Yes, I overdid it. But my birds are important to me and someone is killing them. Lucinda has been checking on them for me. You remember my friend, she's the one who handed me my spyglass the day I twisted my ankle. The point is, Romeo and Juliet are dead. So are Marc Anthony and Cleopatra. You must do something about it right away."

"Do you name all your birds as star-crossed lovers?" The girl was obviously a romantic. When receiving her first letter, he'd thought she was asking him to rewrite William Shakespeare's plays. *Romeo and Juliet are dead. This is most alarming. You must do something about it at once.*

He glanced back at his manor house. "Come back to Pembroke Hall with me. Let's talk. I'll have Colliers bring my carriage around to drive you home afterward."

However, he still made no move to take her arm or to take her *in* his arms. Nor did he offer his arm to her in escort. He didn't trust himself to behave with this girl. Touching her was not a good idea.

Indeed, it was a very bad and dangerous idea.

He forced himself to keep his distance, reminding himself not to allow his attraction to this little nuisance to affect his judgement.

He led her into his library and rang for Bigbury to bring refreshments. Prudence's eyes were shadowed with pain as she took her seat, but a little discomfort did not stop her from soaking in her surroundings. "Your Grace, your home is beautiful, the little of it I've seen."

He nodded and settled behind his desk. "I'll give you a tour of the entire house if you're up to it after we speak."

She laughed and shook her head. "You don't know women very well if you believe any of us would ever pass up a chance to tour your palatial home. I'm no exception. I look forward to it."

He waited for Bigbury to set down a tea tray and some ginger cakes on his desk. Bigbury then poured a cup of tea for Prudence. "That will be all," Bhrodi intoned, casting the man an impatient look. "Stop grinning and close the door behind you."

He then turned to Prudence, knowing he had to get to the business at hand. "Tell me, Miss Pertwee," he said, rising from his seat to come around to the front of his desk while she placed a slice of ginger cake on her plate. "Which cave has caught your notice?"

"It's the one where Romeo and Juliet nested." She nibbled her lip in obvious distress. "Marc Anthony and Cleopatra took it over the following day and they died next. Those villains even killed their hatchlings. Why would anyone do something so cruel? Our local smugglers would never harm those birds. This is the work of contemptible outsiders."

"So that's why you think these are not local smugglers? No local man would be cruel to your birds?" He folded his arms over his chest and rested his hip against the front of his desk, eager to stay close to Prudence and listen to what she had to say. Perhaps Bigbury had been right. He ought to have confided in her sooner, but he couldn't risk that she would report all he'd told her in confidence to the ladies in her birdwatching society. He wanted more information out of her before he revealed his concerns about the Mongoose. "Which cave particularly concerns you?"

"The one where these birds were nesting, of course."

"I realize that. I was hoping you'd give me an indication of where it is located." Prudence was wrong about this man being an outsider. This villain was a local man and dangerous. He might have foreigners working for him, but the Mongoose himself was born and bred in Wales. Indeed, right here in Pembroke or nearby.

She took a sip of her tea, then set down her cup and cast him a generous smile. "It's best if I lead you to the cave myself."

"With your injured foot? No. You'll draw me a sketch of it. Or point it out to me on one of my maps." He was frowning again. He couldn't help it. The girl was wreaking havoc on his composure. One look at her and his body became a hot, frenzied mess. It didn't help that her scent was that of lavender and sea foam, clean and intoxicating.

She ought to have smelled of ruffled feathers and bird droppings. But no, she was as tempting as that ginger cake she was ignoring on her plate.

She returned his frown. "You'll never recognize the right cave on your own."

"I don't want you climbing those cliffs. While you are on my property, you are my responsibility."

She was about to take a bite of her ginger cake, but set it back down. "Give me a paper to sign absolving you of all responsibility. That ought to take care of your unfounded concerns."

"They are not unfounded. These men are dangerous, Miss Pertwee."

Her eyes narrowed. "I knew there was something dodgy going on. What are you hiding from me? Are you the mastermind behind this smuggling operation?"

"Of course not."

She struggled to her feet. "Then why won't you let me help you?"

Although she barely came to his shoulder, she was not at all dissuaded by her lesser height. She cleared her throat and spoke to break their stony silence. "Lucinda and I have notebooks filled with drawings of our bird pairs. We draw them on the cliffs. On the beach. We draw whatever we see around them, including whoever happens to be on the beach or the walking trails or in the nearby waters at that time. Would you care to see our sketches?"

He groaned lightly. "Hell, yes."

The girl might have just solved the mystery for him. Bigbury would give him an earful for not taking Prudence into his confidence sooner.

She cast him a victorious smile. "I thought you might be interested."

He gazed down at this girl with the sparkling jade green eyes. "I owe you an apology, Prudence."

She inhaled lightly. "You called me Prudence. Does this mean we are friends?"

It was safer not to like this girl, but he'd lost that battle long ago. He'd just been too stubborn to admit it to himself until now. "Yes, I think we might be. You may call me Bhrodi when we are alone, but you must never refer to me thus when we are in company. Is that understood?"

"Yes. Quite well understood... Bhrodi." She cast him the softest smile, sweet and openhearted, that only made him feel worse for being so hard on her when her purpose was innocent and she only meant to do good. But those villains had already made two attempts on his life and quickly escaped, each time seeming to disappear into thin air. They had probably run into one of those caves along the cliffs, knowing he did not have enough men necessary to conduct a thorough search.

There were hundreds of caves carved out among the rocks and so much smuggling activity going on under cover of night that no one had any idea who belonged and who were the assassins craftily blending in with the crowd.

However, Prudence knew.

He needed to get whatever information he could out of her, and then put distance between them in order to keep her out of harm's way.

So why had he allowed her to call him Bhrodi?

"I'm not devoid of manners," she continued. "Or common sense, for that matter. I'd be ruined if anyone ever heard me address you with such familiarity. They would immediately assume that you'd seduced me. It is commonly believed that you have only to look at a girl with that seductive gaze of yours to put her under your serpent spell." She gave a little snort and rolled her eyes. "It's a good thing you'd never look at me that way."

He arched an eyebrow. "Why wouldn't I?"

"I talk too much, for starters. I constantly vex you. Men like you prefer women who are obedient and never speak up unless they are asked for their opinion. Something you would never do because you obviously don't trust women."

"That is not true, Prudence. I…" He racked his brain trying to think of the last time he'd turned to a female for answers. His mother. His sisters. But who had he trusted outside of the women in his family?

Prudence cast him a smug grin. "See. You like your conquests to be empty-brained and as bland as boiled leeks."

"Now who is the one giving women a bad name? Being obedient does not mean one's brains are made of boiled leeks. I like to think of an obedient woman as someone helpful, considerate. Someone who is as sweet as honey."

"And what am I then? Brine and vinegar?"

"That you are." He laughed and crossed his arms over his chest. "But so are my mother and my sisters, so you are in good company. I often turn to them for counsel. I know they will tell me the truth, whether or not I like what I hear. For that reason, I very much respect their opinions."

Prudence groaned lightly. "I often club you over the head with the truth."

"Indeed, you do. But you can't help yourself. You don't know how to be anything other than passionate in your opinions." He leaned forward and regarded her quite seriously. "I respect that about you, although you think I don't."

"So you would never seduce me because you respect me?"

He grinned. "Not to mention, your father is the local magistrate."

She nodded. "That too. Why, he might lock you in his prison and throw away the key."

"Or demand that I marry you." Why had he just said that? In all his years of training to become a proper duke, one thing had been drummed into his head before he was old enough to cut his first teeth. Never mention the word 'marry' or any variation thereof to a female unless you intend to make her your wife.

He knew that rule well.

He'd lived by it for almost thirty years.

How had that word slipped out now? In conversation with Prudence Pertwee, no less.

She nibbled her lip in obvious dismay. That forbidden word must have distressed her as well. "Yes, I suppose he would demand marriage. But you'd refuse him because you're one of the most powerful dukes in the realm and I'm… a dotty bird lady. Then I'd be left on my own with a ruined reputation."

"Indeed, you are dotty about your birds. But that aside, what makes you think I would refuse him?"

Her laugh was more of a sputtered guffaw that slowly died out when she noticed he wasn't laughing along with her. "Are you serious? You would agree to marry me?"

She gazed up at him in wonder.

She was standing too close.

Perhaps he was the one who'd moved too close to her. He loved the way her eyes sparkled whenever she looked at him. "I would consider it if I ever seduced you."

She eased back and emitted a sigh that sounded very much like one of relief. "That's a big 'if', isn't it? You scared me for a moment. Can you imagine us together? Well, I suppose it would be lots of fun for me. I'd be your duchess and that would allow me to walk about your property any time I wished. I could study my birds whenever I wanted to. It would be a perfect solution, come to think of it."

"What do you mean?"

"I haven't been raised to enter Society. I wouldn't know what to do. You would have to keep me shut away here while you went off and did whatever an important duke does whenever he's in London. But you'd be married to me, so you wouldn't have to worry about being trapped into marriage by a scheming fortune hunter. You'd go about your business and I'd do the same. I'd enjoy being left behind to study my birds. We'd both get what we wanted."

"How so? I thought you meant to marry only for love."

"I do. I..." Her face suffused with color. She appeared to stop breathing.

Blessed saints!

Was she in love with him?

She tore out of the room before he had the chance to ask. She'd left her walking stick behind, taking off as though a raging fire was about to envelop her and she was fleeing for her life.

He strode out after her, knowing she wouldn't get far without her walking stick. She'd already tired herself out walking up here from town. He caught up to her not far from his home as she was cutting across a nearby copse of trees and already limping.

He grabbed her by the waist and drew her up against him, wrapping his arms around her body and holding her tight to keep her from struggling. "Prudence, I'm not letting you get away. Stop fighting me."

"Please let me go, Your Grace. Have I not humiliated myself enough?"

He turned her to face him, noting the hot tears spilling onto her cheeks. "My name is Bhrodi. I gave you permission to call me Bhrodi."

"That was before you knew how I felt about you. I'm so dense. I never realized it until last week when I sprained my ankle and you had to lift me into your arms. I came undone." She said the last with a quiet sob, using the back of her hand to rub away the moisture on her cheeks. "My insides turned to pudding. My heart... well, it still hasn't recovered."

He released her suddenly and stepped back, raking a hand through his hair. "Don't tell me that."

"I can't help it," she said with a sniffle, once again using her hand to wipe away the stray tears. "I don't know how to be anything but truthful."

He shook his head and gave a mirthless laugh. "I know. You are too often brutally honest with me."

She cast him a pained smile. "You often leave me no choice. You're quite highhanded, even for a powerful and arrogant duke. However, I will admit that I can be the same, at times."

"Certainly when it comes to protecting your birds." He wanted to reach out and take her into his arms again, but knew it would only make matters worse. He liked Prudence's strong will and independent spirit.

He could resist his attraction to this girl when she was fearless and determined. But she now stood before him so innocent and vulnerable. This softer Prudence, this girl who trusted him with the secrets of her heart, was devastating to his resolve. If he took her into his arms now, he would never let her go. "Prudence, I didn't have to carry you in my arms that day. Did it ever occur to you that I wanted to do it? That despite your constant defiance and every other quality about you that I found insufferably irritating, that I wanted you? Did that ever occur to you?"

Her eyes were wide as saucers. "No, quite frankly. It didn't."

He shook his head and gave a groaning laugh.

Her hand went to her throat and she let out a soft gasp. "Are you suggesting that you love me?"

"No, Prudence. Good grief, where did you get that idea? Lustful desire is not the same as love."

She regarded him with confusion. "Then you desire me? Even though I'm as thorny as a bramble bush?"

He nodded. "But I'll never act upon that desire."

"Why not?"

Hell, he wouldn't act upon it because what he felt was something much more than that. He couldn't possibly love her. She was just as she'd said, all brambles and sharp thorns. But he wanted her with an ache that he'd never felt for anyone before. An agonizing ache, if he wished to be honest about it. Which he didn't. He was the Serpent's scion, not some pasty-faced romantic. He controlled his heart. How could he surrender it to Prudence? "I respect you too much to dishonor you. To seduce you would also dishonor your family. Your father is a good man. One of the few honest men around."

"I know. I'm very proud of him. I wish to find a way to make him proud of me."

The soft quiver of uncertainty in her voice tugged at Bhrodi's soul. "I'm sure he is, Prudence. You have many commendable qualities. You are clever and compassionate, for starters. You fight for the things that matter to you. I admire that about you, even though it often puts us at odds."

She cast him a hopeful glance. "Thank you. You're the first man besides my father who's ever told me that. Perhaps this is why I fell in love with you despite your attempts to toss me off your property. You see beyond my outward appearance. You think of my intelligence as a strength and not as a flaw to be subdued. It feels nice to be seen for the person I am and not to be broken and twisted into somebody I'm not."

Hell, she was doing it again, destroying his resistance. She would surely conquer his serpent heart if he ever let down his guard. "You can't blame others for admiring your beauty. It is hard to overlook. I also like that you don't rely on your looks to get your way. In truth, I'm not certain you realize just how beautiful you are."

She cleared her throat. "Are you certain you don't like me enough to marry me? Because it sounds as though you might. Would you give it additional consideration? It would mean a lot to me if you did."

"Are you proposing to me, Prudence?"

Her cheeks turned crimson. "I suppose it must have sounded that way."

"I don't mind that you did. But what I wish to know is whether you proposed because you love me or because you love your birds more and wish to save them?" Why wasn't he ranting and raging and angry at this girl who didn't have the sense to realize that one did not propose to a duke. One waited for the duke to propose. Which he wasn't going to do. Dukes did not offer for magistrate's daughters.

"Why can't I love you and my birds? Must I choose one over the other?"

No, of course not.

Why were they even speaking of love? Worse, speaking of marriage. They had smugglers to catch. He needed to destroy the Mongoose.

He needed to keep Prudence away from that villain and safe.

"Prudence, no more of this romantic nonsense. Do not let your guard down around me. While I may recognize your other fine qualities and have held off out of respect for you, my feelings toward you are not honorable."

"They're not?"

"Not in the least. I want to kiss you. I want to take you into my bed and hold you in my arms. I want to keep you in my bed and bury myself in your delectable body. But I want to do those things to you because you rouse my base desires. Don't mistake my lust for love."

He'd spoken with outrageous bluntness and would not have blamed her if she'd slapped him. The notion did not appear to have crossed her mind. She smiled wryly at him instead. "I won't make that mistake. In truth, I never have and never will. But I'm not certain that all you feel for me is lust. What if you do love me back?"

He growled low in his throat. Why did this girl always have to push him to his limit? "I don't."

"I think you're wrong. Do you wish to know why I think you love me back?"

"No."

Her smile faded in disappointment, but she was obviously not ready to give up. "Very well. I won't tell you. I'll keep quiet about it and not say another word. However, it is a terrible shame that–"

"Prudence, you're still talking." He lifted her into his arms because she was limping and her leg appeared about to buckle out from under her. He couldn't bear to see her in pain. He wanted to protect this girl. He knew he would give up his life without a moment's hesitation to protect her.

But it didn't mean he loved her.

Serpents did not fall in love with bird ladies.

That he wanted to crush his lips to hers, to kiss her and taste her until he'd satisfied himself of his craving for Prudence, did not mean he loved her. That he wanted to feel her soft curves beneath him when he took her into his bed and settled his body over hers, merely proved he was craven in his desires.

He did want to explore every inch of her lithe body. He did want to run his hands and lips along her silken skin until she was writhing with pleasure and calling out his name. He ached to touch her and taste her and spend himself inside of her.

But to do so outside of marriage would crush the life and spirit out of Prudence.

He'd never forgive himself for that.

He wanted to do all of those things to her, but he would do them only in his dreams. Of course, he could have sated his lust elsewhere. He had only to cast a glance and a dozen women would eagerly come to him. But he didn't want other women. He wanted the woman with flame-red hair and jade green eyes who filled his wildest fantasies.

No other.

He couldn't believe it.

Prudence?

But what he felt for Prudence was exactly as she'd suggested, something more than lust. No one but Prudence was ever going to satisfy that feeling. It wasn't love. It couldn't be. Love grew slowly and over great lengths of time, didn't it? Love did not strike as swiftly and lethally as a serpent's bite.

That would be quite the ironic jest, the Serpent caught unaware by love's swift bite.

"I'll take you home," he grumbled. "I need to look at your bird sketches."

He hoped those drawings would reveal the identity of the Mongoose.

His life would then be simplified.

Destroy the Mongoose.

Then close up Pembroke Hall and return to London.

Then try like hell to forget Prudence.

CHAPTER FOUR

"**M**Y NOTEBOOKS ARE gone," Prudence said, hurrying back downstairs to her parlor where Bhrodi had been pacing ever since their arrival. She ought to be thinking of him as His Grace or the Duke of Pembroke. But he'd captured her heart and she couldn't think of him as anything but Bhrodi now.

Her Bhrodi.

Assuming he'd ever admit he felt the same way about her.

It was unlikely.

He was perfection.

She was the irritating bird lady who'd trespassed on his land.

Her heart pounded through her ears. "Someone has been through my bedchamber. They've searched everywhere and ransacked my bureau. That's where these notebooks are supposed to be."

Bhrodi's eyes darkened and he cast her a familiar

frown. "Are you certain? Perhaps you moved them and simply forgot."

"No, I didn't. Someone took them." She rushed into the hall and went in search of Eleanora, finding her and several maids tidying up her father's library. There were empty glasses everywhere and the chairs had been moved around. "Eleanora, was Father here?"

"Why, yes. With members of the town council. They left only a few moments before you returned home. What's the matter, Prudence? You look overset."

"My notebooks are missing."

Eleanora's fat, grayish curls bobbed around her ears as she shook her head in dismissal. "You must have moved them and forgotten," she said, repeating Bhrodi's comment.

"I didn't. I am always careful with these sketch books. Who was here with Father?"

Eleanora motioned for the maids to leave them when Bhrodi entered the library to join the discussion. "Your Grace." She bobbed a respectful curtsy.

"Good afternoon, Mrs. Pertwee. It is important for us to know who accompanied your husband."

"Well, most of the town council was just here. Let

me see," she said, her voice high pitched as her nerves got the better of her. "There was Squire Bennett. My nephew, Joshua Crompton. He took over my first husband's seat on the council. He's a charming young man and quite besotted with Prudence." She paused to frown lightly at Prudence. "I do wish you'd give him a chance."

Bhrodi cleared his throat. "Who else, Mrs. Pertwee?"

"Oh, yes. Sir Reginald Hawley. There was also the blacksmith, Charles Frayne. Oh, and Sir Emrys de Courcy and his son, Dylan de Courcy."

"Lucinda's father and brother," Prudence explained. "But they must be ruled out. Why would they want my notebooks? Lucinda has her own."

Bhrodi's expression turned thoughtful, for he was obviously running through the names in his head, hoping to discern who belonged and who was out of place. "Only those men?"

"Yes, Your Grace. Oh, dear me. I almost forgot. There were two other gentlemen that Sir Emrys and his son brought along, but I did not recognize them. They weren't local men. I'd never seen them before. Now, what were their names?" She shook her head and pursed her lips. "Oh, dear. I can't recall. But I think they were from Aberystwyth. No, that isn't quite right. No, but it was Aber... something?"

She sighed and shook her head again before continuing. "Not very nice men, if you ask me. They were standing in the parlor while the council members were discussing something or other, no doubt concerning them. But I overheard them talking to each other. I couldn't quite make it out. They were whispering. That's when they mentioned Aber... something."

Bhrodi's gaze intensified. "Aberffraw?"

"Yes, it could very well have been. Indeed, it was Aberffraw. I'm sure of it. But that's all I heard, Your Grace. As I said, they weren't friendly chaps. What have they to do with Prudence's lost books?"

Bhrodi shook his head. "I don't know. Perhaps nothing. Did those two strangers ever leave the parlor? Or mention anything else to you?"

Eleanora shook her head. "Leave the parlor? I don't think so, but I was attending to my household duties and not paying particular attention to the council members or those men." Eleanora's expression turned into one of dismay. "I did hear someone go up the stairs, but I assumed it was my husband. Oh, dear. I ought to have looked, but I thought nothing of it at the time."

"Eleanora, you've been most helpful." Prudence patted her hand to calm her as she became agitated. "Please don't distress yourself."

Eleanora nodded and then turned to Bhrodi. "I'm sure my husband will know more about these men. Or Lucinda's father may be of help. I think he and Dylan returned to their house after the meeting ended. They did not follow the others back to the magistrate's hall so they ought to be at home now."

Prudence rushed to the window and glanced across the garden to the neatly maintained house behind her own. She and Lucinda often cut across the grassy expanse instead of using the road whenever visiting each other. "Let's pay a call on them right now. I wonder if Lucinda is home. We must warn her before her books are stolen."

The duke nodded. "Lead the way, Miss Pertwee."

Prudence tried not to look as eager as she felt. Bhrodi always managed to look so calm, but she was leaping out of her skin with excitement to solve this mystery. She had to find out who was killing her birds. She'd leave it up to him to address the matter of smuggling. She didn't care about that. Everyone in Wales smuggled goods or was related to someone who did. It was a harmless enough way of exerting independence over their English dominance.

What was not harmless was the murder of her birds.

She led the way to the de Courcy residence. "What is the significance of that name you mentioned? Aberffraw? Isn't that the name of the old Welsh ruling family? But the House of Aberffraw died out in the late thirteenth century when Llywelyn ap Gruffud was defeated by your English king."

"My king? He is yours as well. Wales has been a part of England ever since that victory." He paused a moment in his step and held her back as they neared the de Courcy home. "Do you still consider yourself Welsh and not English?"

She tipped her chin up. "Should I forget my heritage? Are you any less at fault for thinking of yourself as English when your title is one of the oldest and proudest in Wales? Pembroke means land's end. That's what the dukes of Pembroke were installed to protect. This land. You were the first line of defense from attack by sea. From any foreign force that attempted to step onto the green hills of Wales. Your ancestor was the Serpent. The bravest defender Wales ever had."

"I know my family history." He furrowed his brow in thought. "Tell me about the de Courcy family. Do they feel as you do? They've kept their Welsh names. Father and son. The father's name, Emrys, means immortal in the old Welsh tongue. The son's name, Dylan, means son of the waves."

Prudence's eyes narrowed. "What are you suggesting? That they are traitors to the Crown? We all have pride in our lineage. It doesn't mean we seek to overthrow the English king."

She searched his expression and gasped. "This is why you're really here. This is why you don't want me on those cliffs. You think there's a plot afoot to do just that. But why attempt to overthrow the royal family here? Why not in London? Or is this plot merely a fight to toss the English out of Wales? Does it extend beyond our borders?"

"I don't know," he said quietly. "That's what I need to find out. I don't know who is behind this treachery. But your sketches may contain a vital clue."

He turned and took the final steps to reach the de Courcy front door.

Prudence's heart tugged as she realized the impossibility of her situation. Bhrodi was not of her world. He was a powerful duke with royal connections to one of the oldest ruling houses of Wales as well as England. De Sherra and de Wolfe. Why would he ever admit to loving her, the local bird watcher? To hold out hope that he would was pointless and foolish. "What will we do if those scoundrels have already grabbed Lucinda's sketches?"

He shrugged his shoulders. "I don't know. I'll have to rely on you to tell me what you and Lucinda drew and you'll have to show me the cave in question." He glanced at her foot and frowned as the de Courcy butler opened the door in response to his knock. "You're still limping."

She ignored the pain in her foot. Her birds were more important than any minor discomfort. "I'll manage," she hastily muttered. "You'll just have to help me along the slippery parts."

He grunted, not satisfied with her response. "A bad idea. You already need my help just to walk twenty paces."

She did not bother to contradict him since Warfield was looking at them and obviously wondering what they were going on about. "Good afternoon, Your Grace. Miss Prudence."

Prudence smiled at the kindly, older man. "Warfield, is Miss Lucinda at home?"

Warfield moved aside to allow them both in. "No, Miss Prudence. She walked to the cliff caves to study your birds this morning and has not yet returned." He frowned lightly. "She said that she was going to meet you there. Did you not see her?"

Prudence cast Bhrodi a worried glance. "Meet me? Are you certain she mentioned me and not one of our other birdwatching friends?"

"She held up a note and distinctly said that you had sent it with instructions to meet her at your usual spot, Llangolyn Rock." His eyes widened in alarm. "Did you not instruct her to bring her sketch books too? She walked out with a travel bag in hand that she said contained those books."

Prudence tamped down her own alarm. "What else did the note say?"

"That's all she mentioned to me." The blood appeared to drain from the poor man's face. "We must alert Sir Emrys and Master Dylan immediately. I believe they are still with your father."

Prudence placed a comforting hand on the butler's arm. "We thought they'd returned here. But we must have been mistaken. Warfield, I'm sure it's all been a silly misunderstanding that will quickly be cleared up. We'll find Miss Lucinda's father and brother. As you said, they must still be with my father. Even if they're not, their meeting just broke up so they can't have gone far."

She also knew that Bhrodi would put all his resources at their disposal to find Lucinda, assuming there was cause for alarm. She noticed that his jaw was clenched and his serpent eyes were dark with concern.

As soon as they were away from Lucinda's house, he wasted no time in finding Colliers and issuing him instructions. "Alert Miss Pertwee's father, but be discreet about it. I don't want Sir Emrys de Courcy or others to know what's going on yet."

Prudence gasped. "You're not going to tell Lucinda's father that she might be missing?"

"No," he said with a sharp authority that momentarily stilled her tongue. "If de Courcy brought those strangers here, he might be involved in this plot against the Crown. His son as well."

"Not Dylan!" she said in a harsh whisper, not wishing any passers by to overhear.

"Perhaps Lucinda, too. Inadvertently, no doubt. She might have been obeying her father's instructions. Unlike you, she seems the sort to obey without questioning."

Prudence didn't know what to say. This was too much. She loved Lucinda like a sister. The de Courcy family and hers were the closest of friends. It had to be a mistake and she would do all in her power to prove it.

Bhrodi was no longer staring at her, but had turned away to quietly finish giving orders to Colliers. "You'll likely find them both at the magistrate's hall. Miss Pertwee and I will go straight to Llangolyn Rock. Find out what you can about the de Courcys and the two strangers who were with them today. Afterward, go straight to Pembroke Hall and alert Bigbury. Both of you are to join us at Llangolyn Rock."

Bhrodi turned to Prudence when they were once more alone. "In truth, I doubt we'll find Lucinda there. But it's the best place to start. Can you walk?"

She nodded. Even if she couldn't, she'd never admit it. If Lucinda was in danger, she'd crawl on her knees the entire way if she had to in order to save her best friend.

Bhrodi glanced at her leg and then toward cliff road. "My carriage will be useless on these narrow trails."

"You needn't worry about me, Bhrodi. I will manage." It still felt odd calling him that aloud. Odd and intimate. But his feelings for her weren't important now. Finding Lucinda was all that mattered. "What about the two strangers who were with my father and the de Courcys?"

"If they are involved in this intrigue, I'm sure they fled the moment they noticed my carriage in town. Colliers and Bigbury will track them down later. Saving your friend is our first priority, assuming she's in any danger. Then I need you to show me the cave you were talking about."

Prudence nodded. "I have chills running up and down my spine. I can't shake off this feeling of dread. What if those sinister strangers harmed Lucinda? Their presence here is too much of a coincidence."

"Don't be too hasty to condemn them," Bhrodi cautioned. "We have no proof that anything out of the ordinary has occurred. For all we know, Lucinda might be skipping back to town as we speak… or has run off on an assignation and used you as her cover."

Prudence regarded him aghast. "How dare you consider such a notion! Why would you suggest such a thing?"

"Because she has a travel bag with her. Telling her butler that she carried her sketch books would provide a reasonable explanation for her walking out with that bag. She only held up a piece of paper and waved it about for effect, but never gave it to Warfield to read. He merely repeated what she'd told him. For all we know, her books are safely in her bedchamber and she could be–"

"Don't you dare suggest that she eloped with a beau. I'd know if Lucinda had one. She'd never keep that secret from me. I'm certain something nefarious is afoot." The bad feeling had settled in the pit of Prudence's stomach and would not go away.

Bhrodi gave a curt nod. "We'll search the promontory and caves first, and then search Lucinda's bedchamber for those books afterward. You're with me now and can tell me most of what's in those drawings anyway."

They made their way hurriedly out of town. Prudence led him along the familiar path that she and her birdwatching friends had taken for years without incident.

She tried to move fast, but her sore foot would not cooperate. She knew that she was holding Bhrodi back. His frustration was palpable. So was hers. She felt like a snail inching slowly up the hill, every lost moment precious. "Do you think those villains have abducted her?"

Her greatest fear was that they'd find Lucinda dead, her broken body lying at the base of one of the cliffs. She hoped those strangers hadn't stolen her sketch books and then pushed her off.

But if they had abducted her, intending to hold her for ransom, then there was still hope of saving her friend.

Tears welled in Prudence's eyes. She quickly wiped them away with her sleeve, blaming her watery eyes on the biting wind that swept off the sea and howled up the cliff face. She didn't want Bhrodi sending her back to town because she was too overset.

He took her hand and helped her up the last hill. Llangolyn Rock came into view. She was about to call out for her friend, but Bhrodi stopped her. He reached into his boot and withdrew a small pistol. Prudence gasped when he handed it to her. "What's this for?"

"Your protection. Wait here and stay out of sight until I tell you it's safe to come up. Understood?"

She nodded.

After what could only have been a few moments, but seemed endless, Bhrodi returned to her side and took her hand in his to help her up onto the overlook. "She hasn't been here. No sign of a struggle either. In truth, no sign that anyone was up here today."

Prudence attempted to hand him back the pistol, but he shook his head. "No, hold on to it for now. You might need it later."

"That sounds ominous."

"No, just cautious." He glanced around once more. The wind whipped through his dark hair, but the tousled look only made him appear handsomer than she already thought him. Sunlight shone down upon them, and for a moment, Prudence thought that he did resemble a mythical god brought down from the heavens in a golden chariot.

"Prudence," he said with a throaty rumble, "look around. Do you see anything that I might have missed? Do you ever leave notes for each other here? In a secret place? Under a rock or in the knothole of a nearby tree?"

She shook her head. "No. Nothing like that. We were always together and had no need." But she scanned carefully for a sign of her friend having been here. She knew this area very well and would have noticed if something appeared to be out of place.

All was as it should be.

But one last thing worried her. "Bhrodi," she said in a ragged whisper so that her voice was almost lost upon the fleeting wind. "Look below. I can't bring myself to do it."

He stepped close and wrapped his arms around her, understanding her fear. "Prudence, rest easy. I did that before I called you up here." He did not need to say the rest aloud, for he'd just assured her that her friend's body was not lying in a broken heap at the bottom of the cliff.

"Thank goodness." She clung to him while fighting to control her tears of relief. She had to remain composed and subdue the rush of feelings that rose like stormy waves inside of her, swelling and crashing against the tender wall of her heart.

It wasn't easy to remain calm when she was still so frightened for her friend.

Lucinda wasn't here.

So where was she?

CHAPTER FIVE

BHRODI HELD ON to Prudence, telling himself that this is what she needed and ignoring the fact that he wanted her in his arms with a desperate ache. She looked to him for comfort and he wanted to provide all he could.

But they both knew that Lucinda could still be in danger.

He prayed that his first thought was correct, that she had run off with some besotted foolscap to marry against her father's wishes. It was the sort of thing a young woman who believed herself in love might do. Lucinda was just the sort of girl a young man would fall in love with, too. Pretty. Not too taxing on the brain.

Not at all like Prudence, although Prudence was certainly beautiful. Jaw dropping, heart stopping beautiful, in truth. But she could drive a man insane with her questions and causes and spirited mind. She was as fiery as her blazing red hair.

"Sweetheart, she'll be all right." Blast, had he just called her sweetheart? What was wrong with him? He never spouted endearments unless it was to seduce a woman out of her clothes, and he made it a hard and fast rule never to seduce an innocent.

He'd never been tempted to break that rule until Prudence had stormed into his life. "I'm sure she'll be all right," he repeated, admonishing himself for giving her false hope. In his own defense, he sincerely believed that Lucinda was not in any real danger.

Prudence drew away from him to gaze out across the shimmering sea.

Bhrodi moved to stand beside her, but kept a little distance between them. He sensed she needed it.

He did not mind standing here to take in the view. He loved the sight of the sea, the mix of swirling blue water and white foamy caps formed by the breaking waves. He loved the diamond shimmer of the sun glinting upon that endless expanse. Thanks to Prudence, he was even learning to love the various flocks of birds that flew in and out among the jagged cliffs. He was even becoming tolerant of their noisy cries.

These creatures had just been mindless birds to

him before. But now he was noticing their differences and coming to admire their majesty and grace. Prudence's influence. He would soon learn to tell which bird had built which nest. He would soon know which birds lived here all year long and which ones migrated.

He breathed in the breeze that carried the scent of fish and seaweed and rugged beauty along with it. "Point out which cave caught your notice, Prudence. I'm going down there now."

"I'll go down there with you."

"No, you need to stay here." He wanted to throttle her for her strength of spirit, but it was this very thing he admired about her. "Keep alert and hold on to that pistol until Colliers and Bigbury arrive. Tell Colliers and Bigbury where I am. Send Colliers down to me. Bigbury is to remain with you, keeping watch on the trails and cliffs. Tell Bigbury that he is to alert me if you see something out of the ordinary. *You*," he said, emphasizing the word with a frown, "are to stay up here and not go anywhere near that cave."

"Why? Because I'm a suspect?" Her eyes widened in anger.

His narrowed in frustration. "Must you question

everything I say or do? You know you're not a suspect. Indeed, you're one of the few people around here I can trust. I expect your father is also trustworthy."

"He is."

"But you know I cannot completely rule anyone out yet. Once we're done here, I'll pay a call on your father. I need to question him."

That flicker of anger turned fiery. "But you just said he's innocent."

"I sincerely believe he is, but he may know more than he realizes. Certainly about those strangers. Probably about Lucinda's father and brother. In truth, about anyone on the town council. Even the local merchants, farmers, tavern owners. Somehow these plots always seem to take root whenever men are drunk."

She arched an eyebrow. "So I'm to wait here while you investigate on your own? You claim to believe in my innocence, but you've ordered me to keep out of your way."

He sighed. "Prudence, don't be difficult. You aren't trained for espionage. You'll only get hurt and put us all in danger."

"I hate when you state it like that."

A grin finally escaped his lips, for he'd just won this battle. He doubted he'd win many with Prudence. "Why? Because it makes sense?"

She nodded grudgingly and extended her hand to point toward the nearby cliffs. "Do you see where those choughs are circling just above the rocky shore?"

"Yes."

She moved her hand slightly upward and to the right. "See those three caves just above the circling birds?"

"Yes," he repeated.

"The middle cave is the one used by those outside smugglers. The other two caves are not in use. They're situated too low and flood completely when the tide comes in. Smugglers can't store anything in them because the contents would all wash out to sea. But the mouth of that middle cave is just high enough and it has a rocky lip as an added barrier to keep the tide from rushing in." She cleared her throat. "None of the locals will use it because that cave is still situated too low and will flood in a violent storm, especially our many winter storms. I think these particular smugglers are only using it for the short term. They intend to move fast and will have those goods out of there within the next few days."

Bhrodi listened attentively, struggling to keep his grin from broadening. Prudence would have made a first rate agent and he was a horse's arse for not appreciating her knowledge of the terrain or her cleverness. "Go on. Is there more?"

She nodded. "There happens to be a back entrance to that cave. I doubt anyone is aware of it but me. The route to reach it winds along the hills behind this cliff."

"So it would take longer for me to reach the cave."

"Yes, but it is a safer approach. No one has noticed that entry because it's hidden by Romeo and Juliet's nest. You can sneak into the cave unseen by going in that back way, but you'd have to break apart their nest." Her sigh, as she emitted it, was ragged and filled with sadness. "Just be gentle when taking it apart."

Yet again, he stifled the urge to put his arms around her and take her into his embrace. He'd do it later. He had much he wished to say to Prudence, but now was not the time. "I'll climb down the cliff path. There are no boats in this cove and no one is on the beach. It should be safe enough."

She agreed, but had more to say before he began his descent. "Bhrodi, you will come across other caves that are higher up. I would appreciate your not looking into those."

He laughed, for this was a typical Prudence thing to say. She loved her birds, but also deeply cared for the local townspeople and did not want any of them to be caught smuggling. The punishment was dire, if one had a mind to ever enforce the law. "I won't look. I have no interest in disrupting the local businesses."

"Thank you." She placed a hand on his arm to hold him back a moment. "Be careful."

"I always am. They haven't killed me yet."

"Yet?" Her eyes widened and her grip tightened on his arm. "Do you mean to say they've tried before?"

Bollocks.

He sighed as he removed his jacket and handed it to her. It would only constrain him as he climbed down the cliff side. "Yes, which is why I want you to hold tight to that pistol. But don't waste your shot. If confronted, aim for the leader's chest. The torso is the biggest target and easiest to hit. If that leader happens to be Lucinda's father, don't falter. He may love you like a daughter, but he'll still kill you."

He left her with her mouth agape and made his way swiftly down toward the caves.

⟫⟫⟫✳⟪⟪⟪

PRUDENCE WANTED TO follow Bhrodi, but dared not.

He'd given her strict instructions not to follow him down.

She had no choice but to respect his wishes. Besides, it was broad daylight. Little activity would take place now. He'd be safe enough even if scoundrels were hiding out in that cave. He was a descendant of the Serpent. He was smart and brave and an experienced agent of the Crown.

But she knew those caves better than anyone else.

She set his jacket out upon one of the overhanging rocks and then stretched flat atop it while peering down to follow his progress. She knew he'd easily manage the cliff trail, for he was as surefooted as she was and certainly much stronger.

Still, she breathed a sigh of relief when he reached the bottom and had only to make his way across the rocks below that middle cave. The tide was out, so there was little chance of him getting soaked by the constant waves that lapped the shore. But the tide came in quickly around here.

Oh, dear. Did he know that?

She had neglected to mention it.

"He must know it," she muttered to herself. After all, he was the Duke of Pembroke. His family had ruled over these acres for hundreds of years. Pembroke was in his blood. Surely the ebb and flow of the sea was as familiar to him as the beating of his heart.

But what if it wasn't?

That middle cave would not flood, but he'd be forced to swim to land once he was out of it because all the rock footholds would be underwater.

Did he know how to swim? She expected so. He would have given some indication if he didn't. Perhaps cast a worried glance or asked her how high the water level rose. She shook her head to dismiss the notion. Bhrodi had no weaknesses. He made everything look easy, no matter how difficult the task was for others to accomplish.

But these small worries continued to nag at her, until they suddenly gained in importance as a party of men rowed their vessel into the cove. She hadn't noticed them until now because their boat had been hidden behind one of the jutting cliff faces. "Oh, no. Bhrodi."

They were rowing toward the very cave that Bhrodi had just entered and was now exploring.

She scrambled off the outcropping before any of those blackguards noticed her. Where were Bigbury and Colliers? She had been ordered to wait for them, but that was before Bhrodi realized he would be in imminent danger. She dared not delay and wait for his men to arrive. But she could leave them a clue.

Quickly smoothing an area of dirt with the palm of her hand, she drew a map to lead them to the cave by the back entrance hidden under Romeo and Juliet's nest. She would take this route herself now. It was longer than the cliff trail, but there was no help for it. Those men in the boat would immediately spot anyone attempting to climb down the trail along the face of the cliff.

She left the duke's jacket behind.

She didn't need it and it would only hamper her. In any event, his men would see it and know they'd been there.

However, she took the pistol he'd given her earlier.

She'd never used one before.

Could she kill a man?

She wasn't certain.

Perhaps she could if it meant saving Bhrodi's life.

Yes, she'd kill a man for that.

CHAPTER SIX

B HRODI ENTERED THE cave and was immediately swallowed in its tomb-like blackness. There had to be candles or a lantern close by, he realized, for every smuggler left a means of illumination near the entrance to his hideout.

He quickly found the means – a single lantern – along with the matches to be used for it.

Wasting no time, he moved behind a stack of boxes and then lit the precious source of light, careful to remain behind those boxes so that the orange glow it now cast would not be seen in the distance. That it was still daytime and the sun was high above the horizon helped to hide its brilliance. However, someone with sharp eyes would spot the light and know something was amiss.

He had to move fast to find what he needed and get out of here.

He knew how to operate swiftly and silently, but

the cave had been carved from ancient storms and thousands of years of pounding waves. It was now shaped in such as way as to exaggerate all sound. His every footstep, his every breath, resounded off the dank cave walls. The boxes piled high ought to have muffled the sound, but did little to alleviate the noise.

The cave was cool and its rock floor was covered in slime since sunlight never reached inside to burn away the moss and molds that grew at will within the crevices. The cave grew colder the deeper he went inside, until it was almost cold enough for his breath to mist when he inhaled and exhaled. He kept walking, following the sound of steadily rushing water that emanated from somewhere along the rear cave wall. No doubt a small waterfall that had developed over the years and would eventually collapse that wall.

He glanced toward the entrance, listening carefully to the softly pounding waves that broke along the rocks below the mouth of the cave. The tide was coming in, which meant the rocks he'd used as stepping stones would soon be covered by the sea.

He had to work fast.

He searched for Lucinda first. Although he doubted that she had been abducted, there was always the chance she had been and was tied up here. But he found no sign of her, nor was there any sign that someone had been kept here. "Thank goodness," he muttered, the sound of his voice immediately picked up and resounding off the rock walls.

Next, he strode to the back of the cave and held up the lantern while he searched for the hidden entry that was covered by the bird's nest. He lost a few more precious moments in finding it, but it was too important to overlook. He needed that back way out if the tide came in faster than expected or if the villains made an unexpected appearance.

Now satisfied that he had located his route of escape, he began to crack open the wooden crates piled high against the back wall.

"Bollocks," he muttered, realizing there were crest markings on each crate. Three eagles. The emblem of the defeated Welsh princes. So this was more than a madman seeking revenge on him. This was confirmation that the Mongoose intended to lead an incipient Welsh rebellion against English rule.

But who was the Mongoose? And who else in Pembroke was a part of his scheme?

The de Courcy men and those strangers they'd

brought to their council meeting? Did they have any local support? Or were they hoping to rouse the locals into a frenzy once their rebellion started?

And what was their claim to authority?

Was one of them a descendant of a king of Wales?

He searched the boxes thoroughly. Some contained rifles. Others contained gunpowder. Others contained miscellaneous munitions and weaponry including crossbows. He used the butt of one of those rifles to break the springs on the crossbows. Why store the weaponry here and not closer to Caernarfon Castle? Were these traitors planning to invade the south of Wales by sea? But who was to help them? Napoleon had been defeated at Waterloo. The French were not going to invade. Nor were the Irish, although a mad Welshman could always gain the support of a few Irishmen who wished to cause mischief.

Any invasion was doomed to fail. At best it would be a symbolic gesture.

Of course, killing him, a blood descendant of the Serpent, would be the potent symbol they would need for all Welshmen to take notice. That's why they were so doggedly after him. They had to kill him, for he was the current Duke of Pembroke. The defender of Wales.

The Serpent who would strike down all usurpers of the Crown.

He next moved to destroy their gunpowder. It was a simple enough matter to accomplish. He rolled several kegs filled with the black powder toward the back wall and placed them under the small waterfall. He popped off the lids and watched the water thoroughly soak through the powder.

He grabbed more kegs and did the same.

There were too many to finish the task before the tide rolled in.

He left the rest, knowing he'd done enough for now. His message would be sent to the perpetrators.

He started toward the mouth of the cave, but had taken no more than a step before he heard voices. *Bollocks.* What were these men doing here? It wasn't anywhere near nightfall yet. Which meant they were afraid their plot had been uncovered and were scrambling to act now. Or perhaps they were making a hasty retreat?

He doused his lantern, set it atop one of the boxes, and then moved silently toward the bird's nest that hid the rear escape. The access out was more of a narrow tunnel that was covered by the nest. He reached up and grabbed onto the lip of the tunnel to pull himself through it. His shoulders were as broad as the circular hole and scraped along the rock edges as he forced his way upward.

He paid no mind to the cuts and scratches he was receiving, more concerned that no loose pebbles fell and resounded through the cave to alert them of his presence. Carefully bracing himself along the tunnel walls, he made his toward the top, not daring to breathe until his palm touched twigs and other debris used to form the nest.

He'd reached the top.

He gave one more to push to topple the nest and hoist himself out.

The sea breeze felt cool against his cheeks.

The dazzling sun momentarily blinded him, but as his eyes adjusted to the light, he saw Prudence beside the nest. He held back a stream of curses, but she had to know what he was thinking, for his eyes were ablaze and he was furious. "I told you not–"

"I had to warn you about those men." She held his pistol in one hand and grabbed his hand with her free one. "Come this way. They'll see the ray of light and realize there is another entrance to the cave. They'll be through the tunnel at any moment."

"Prudence–"

"Not now, Bhrodi. You can shout at me to your heart's content later. You need to run. I can't. My foot hurts too much. Don't worry about me. I'll hide behind one of the other nests. I'll be all right."

He started to protest, but she cut him off. "They're after you. Not me. They want the Serpent, not a dotty bird lady."

"Who also happens to be the magistrate's daughter. You'd be a useful bargaining chip for them, assuming they don't panic and simply kill you. I'm not leaving you behind. Who knows what those desperate fools might do to you?" He hauled her over his shoulder and took off as fast as he dared. They were still on the cliff, for the nest opening had merely let him out onto one of the many cliff ledges.

The path off that ledge was a narrow trail with the thick cliff wall to one side and a sheer drop onto the rocks and pools of swirling water below on the other.

The tide was now coming in.

If they fell, and the waves flowed in at just the right time, they might survive the fall. But did Prudence know how to swim?

"They're coming through the tunnel," Prudence warned. The fact that she was over his shoulder and facing backward allowed her to serve as a lookout. "Oh, no! They're taking aim at us."

"I'm not worried about them. They're too far away to hit us." But he set her down and forced her behind him, purposely pinning her against the cliff wall as he sheltered her with his body. Where were Bigbury and Colliers? He could use them now.

"If they're too far away to hit us, then why are we stopping?" She grunted as he pressed his back against her to keep her from squirming away and providing a target for the blackguards coming at them from both sides now.

He quickly looked around for any means of escape... short of jumping off this ledge into the water. The jump was still too dangerous to attempt. Any miscalculation on his part and they would hit the jagged rocks.

They were trapped.

The cliff face was too sheer to climb up.

Armed men were approaching from the foot of the path he'd just run up.

More armed men were approaching from the top

of the path, cutting off their escape route. There was nowhere to run. *Bollocks*. They'd have to jump. "Can you swim, Prudence?"

"Yes. Why?"

Lord, the girl was always full of questions. "Because that's what we're going to do."

He fired off a shot and struck one of the men who'd just come up through the nest. Prudence gasped. "I thought you said their shots wouldn't reach us. But yours hit–"

"I lied." He grabbed the pistol he'd given her and fired a shot in the other direction, striking one of the men at the top of the path. That bought them a precious few moments. He waited to the count of three, enough time for the tide to flow in.

He grabbed Prudence's hand. "Hold your breath. We're going in the water," he said just as more shots rang out. One tore along his ribs like wildfire, searing a line of flesh along his chest. But it somehow tore clean through and did not lodge in his body.

"Bhrodi!"

Had one of those shots struck Prudence? He didn't care about himself, all he cared about was saving her. He held tightly onto her hand as they soared off the cliff ledge and hit the cold water with a splash that was lost among the breaking waves.

They both went under and were held under by the crushing force of the ebbing waves. The tide had come in, the water now high enough to completely submerge the rocks that were immediately below their feet.

He grabbed Prudence and drew her up protectively against his body. Even if she knew how to swim, she wouldn't have the muscle to overcome the downward pull of the tide. He wasn't certain that he had the strength either.

He'd been shot.

He couldn't tell how bad the damage was, for his heart was pumping hard and his mind was racing with a battle fervor.

He opened his eyes underwater, ignoring the salty burn of the sea to look around. He saw the tell-tale crimson streak of blood emanating from his chest, winding like a silk ribbon around his body and floating toward Prudence. He hoped the shock of cold water would help to stanch his blood loss, but he didn't know how much he'd already lost or how much he would lose before the bleeding stopped, assuming it ever stopped.

His chest still felt as though it had been set ablaze, the fire burning within him with a hot intensity that not even the cold sea water could completely douse.

He refused to consider the possibility that he might bleed to death.

He had to save Prudence first.

Hugging her against him, he kept her wrapped in his arms as he kicked his legs and swam upward for air, needing only two solid thrusts to accomplish his goal. Their heads broke above the water line at the same time. He heard her soft gasps as she gulped in as much air as her lungs could manage.

He did the same, and once he'd caught his breath enough to speak, he began asking questions. "Prudence, are you all right? Were you hit?" He didn't think so, for he hadn't noticed any streaks of crimson emanating from her body. "Did you break any bones when falling into the water?" He swept his hands along her body, over her every magnificent curve and limb.

"I'm fine, Bhrodi. It's you I'm worried about." She touched his face, as though needing to make certain he was real and still breathing beside her.

He was still running his hands along her body, for he felt the same need to make certain she was unharmed. To hell with all dukes and serpents and villains. To hell with keeping his heart so guarded that this precious girl had no idea how important she'd become to him. He silently vowed that he would touch her again once they were safely back at Pembroke Hall. But that touch would be hot and possessive as he claimed her for his own in the privacy of his bedchamber.

If they ever made it that far.

First, he had to keep them from drowning.

He held onto Prudence as a powerful wave crashed over them, dragging both of them underwater once more and roughly tumbling them forward so that they hit the cliff's rock face. He twisted his body so that he took the brunt of the impact. But he knew that he needed to get a handhold on that rock face before they tired and the next waves swept them out to sea.

All it would take was another powerful wave to sweep them out too far and drown them.

After several tries, he thrust his arm upward in one powerful stroke and finally managed to grab a solid hold on the rock. He ignored the fire that continued to burn in his chest, and lifted Prudence onto a narrow ledge carved out by the pounding waters. But he no longer had the strength to climb up himself. It didn't matter. He only needed to hold on long enough for help to arrive.

Where were Bigbury and Colliers?

Would they know where to search? This little ledge could not be seen from the cliff path. While it would hamper their rescue, it was also to their advantage. He and Prudence might survive, assuming those villains decided to load the boxes onto their boat and escape instead of hunting them down. Surely, those men had to realize their plot was crumbling and they had to retreat before they were captured.

"Bhrodi, let me help you up." Prudence barely had breath left in her and was struggling to brace herself more steadily on the narrow ledge. But that didn't stop her from reaching out to him and trying to pull him up beside her.

"You can't lift me. I'm too big." His words were strained and every gasping breath he took sent a searing heat through his lungs.

"But you were shot. You're bleeding."

"I know, sweetheart." Why had he called her that now? Perhaps because his head was spinning and he was about to black out.

She circled her arms around one of his and grabbed firm hold of his hand. "If you think I'm going to let you slip away from me, you'd better think again. I love you, Bhrodi. I love you with all my heart. I love you more than my precious birds. I love you even though you are a big, arrogant, stubborn, and thoroughly irritating, pigheaded oaf."

How had the word 'love' slipped in among that string of insults?

"I'm going to propose to you again if we ever get out of here alive," she continued, still ignoring the fact that dukes were supposed to do the proposing. But this was Prudence and she operated by her own set of rules. "No lunatic traitor is going to get in the way of that."

She was still talking, for her lips were moving. But Bhrodi's head was now spinning and there was a painful hum in his ears that drowned out all sound. Another wave crashed over him and he did not have the strength left to fight against it. He was now underwater, surrounded by a pool of darkness, but Prudence still had hold of his arm.

She dragged him back up and pressed her mouth firmly to his before he had the chance to catch his breath. Perhaps she thought he'd stopped breathing and was determined to breathe life back into him. Or was it a kiss?

No, it wasn't a proper kiss.

He'd show her how to do it right once they were safely back at Pembroke Hall.

He held onto that thought, for he no longer had the strength to control what was going on and he didn't know what was happening to him. That hum was growing louder and an odd tingling sensation now coursed through his body. Perhaps it was from the feel of Prudence's mouth on his. He loved the soft warmth of her lips against his.

But this tingling sensation did not spring from his desire for Prudence. It represented something more ominous.

Another wave crashed over him.

Water swirled in a violent circle around him and he felt himself slip out of Prudence's grasp once more.

"Bhrodi, hold on!" He felt her hand graze his as she frantically searched for him to drag him upward to safety.

But the grip of the tidal waters was deadly and overpowered him no matter how hard he fought against it. Still, he did not stop trying. As the violent swirls eased for just a moment, he managed to swim to the surface with several powerful thrusts. But he was dealing with a force far mightier than his own.

Ridiculously, his biggest regret had nothing to do with kings or battles or his responsibilities as a duke. No, indeed. His biggest regret was that he hadn't given Prudence a proper kiss.

Or told her that he loved her.

CHAPTER SEVEN

"I 'M NOT LETTING go of you," Prudence repeated each time a wave crashed over Bhrodi's big, unresponsive body. The tide's ebbing force was frighteningly strong, but no force would ever be strong enough to drag him away from her. She would die before ever letting go of him.

Her teeth were chattering and she was shivering.

How long before she lost consciousness?

She refused to think about it. She would hold onto him even though her hands were too numb to feel his muscles and flesh. She would hold on tight, even though her arms were too numb to circle around his broad shoulders and hold his head above the water.

Shooting pains as sharp as lightning bolts now ran up and down her arms, but she ignored them. "Bhrodi. Oh, God. Bhrodi, don't give up."

She hoisted him up as far as she could, which was just enough to get his head above water. His eyes were closed, those beautiful silver orbs that had the power to penetrate her heart with their serpent gaze. His skin was cold and his lips were a dark shade of purple. "Bhrodi, I love you. You can't give up."

The water was a mix of red and blue swirls around his body which meant he was still bleeding.

Blood in the water was a dangerous thing. It attracted all manner of ocean predators.

She'd fight them off if any were drawn to this rocky perch.

She'd fight off every creature imaginable to save him.

But in the next moment, she realized that sea creatures were the least of their worries. The traitors who'd shot Bhrodi were now rowing toward them, no doubt having decided to search for them in order to make certain they were dead.

Of all the bad luck. Why had these men bothered? Wasn't it more urgent for them to pack up their cache of weapons and escape? Was killing Bhrodi more important to them than saving their worthless hides?

"Bhrodi, tell me what to do," she whispered, hoping he was conscious and could hear her.

There was little either of them could do even if he

miraculously recovered his strength in time. So she did the only thing that made sense for her to do. She kissed him with all her heart and soul. She kissed his unresponsive purple lips and cradled him in her arms. "I love you."

She didn't know how she was going to do it, but she would fight until she drew her last breath. It wouldn't be long now. The boat, propelled by a dozen oarsmen, was almost upon them.

Up close, the vessel loomed quite large. It was bigger than she'd realized. In addition to the oars, it had a mast to support one presently furled sail.

She held her head up in a gesture of defiance and gazed steadily at the men standing on its deck. She could make out the faces of several who were peering over the railing and coldly staring back at her.

She recognized one in particular.

Her heart sank.

"Oh, Bhrodi. You were right. He's in it up to his eyeballs."

Bhrodi's eyes abruptly opened wide, alarming her. She gave a soft cry, at first thinking the worst and believing he'd passed away in her arms. But he was still breathing. She felt the steady rise and fall of his chest against her palm, although she was careful not to touch the bloody gash along his chest where he'd been shot. "Do you hear me?"

A low growl emanated from the back of his throat.

What was he doing? Did he know what he was doing?

Something long and slithery suddenly glided past them. Prudence gasped and tried to draw Bhrodi onto the ledge. But he resisted. It wasn't that his body was unresponsive. He was purposely resisting. She couldn't lift him out of harm's way on her own. The creature circled back and glided over Bhrodi, its big, snake body grazing Bhrodi's chest and arms before suddenly turning away from him and swimming toward the boat.

Prudence blinked her eyes and then blinked again, not believing what she was seeing. That creature appeared to grow in size, its long, round body swelling and elongating until it turned into something monstrous.

A sea serpent of myth.

The Serpent.

But that was merely the name given to the dukes of Pembroke because of their silver-gray, snake eyes and their fighting prowess. In battle, their strikes were lethal and quick.

The creature slid under the boat and gave it a *thwack* with its tail so that the keel no longer held the vessel steady and it began to rock violently. The men aboard, so smug a moment ago, now clutched the sides in panic. The creature slid under the boat again, then turned and slammed into it with all its might so that the boat was in danger of tipping over.

Then this serpent slowly turned its enormous body, like that of an ancient leviathan, and once again slammed against the boat with crushing force. It repeated the same action until men began to fall into the water and the boat slowly began to break apart. "Bhrodi, can you see what's happening?"

"I see it, Pru." His gaze never left the sea serpent as it destroyed the vessel until almost nothing was left of it but a massive, sinking deck and floating pieces of driftwood.

A moment later, Bhrodi doubled over as though in pain. But no, he wasn't in pain and that alarmed her all the more. She couldn't be certain because of the noise from the boat splitting open and the men's screams as they fell into the water, but it sounded as though

Bhrodi was still growling like a predator on the attack.

Was he controlling this serpent?

No, it was too ridiculous to consider.

More men fell into the water.

She heard a gut wrenching scream and suddenly the water around the sinking boat turned crimson. Another man screamed in abject fear and then abruptly stopped. Then another. More shrieks that suddenly turned silent. More ominous red swirls appeared in the water as more men disappeared.

"Bhrodi, make it stop." She'd never seen anyone die before. She didn't care that these very men would have killed her and Bhrodi. This was a horrible way to die.

Bhrodi finally managed to pull himself onto the ledge and then drew her into his arms. He held her head against his bleeding chest, his breaths heavy as he spoke words to try and calm her. She couldn't make out what he was saying. The screams of those men were still echoing in her ears long after they'd met their watery deaths.

The boat was submerged now and all that remained visible was its swaying mast upon the glistening water.

Then, it too sank below the surface.

The sun broke through a few passing cloud and

now shone down upon the blue expanse that was deceptively tranquil.

The last two men were swimming toward her, crying out to be saved. Sir Emrys de Courcy and his son, Dylan.

The serpent silently rose up behind them.

"No! Not Lucinda's family." Prudence held out her hand to Dylan.

A sudden wall of water slammed her back against the ledge.

Her head struck the rocks.

A blinding pain shot through her temples and she lost consciousness.

CHAPTER EIGHT

PRUDENCE AWOKE IN an unfamiliar bed.

She attempted to sit up, but fell back with a groan as what felt like a blacksmith's hammer began to pound inside her head. She put a hand to her brow and realized that her hair was dry and splayed long and loose against her elegant pillows. These surroundings were too elegant for the Pertwee household. Where was she? And how was she not dead?

"Prudence, you're finally awake."

She recognized Bhrodi's deep, rumbling voice that was filled with relief and turned to him. "You're alive. Oh, Bhrodi. I was so afraid I'd lost you." She struggled once more to sit up, this time successfully.

"I know, sweetheart. You had me worried, too," he said, his voice still laden with relief, which explained why he'd used the unexpected endearment. *Sweetheart.* She liked the sound of it. He reached out to stroke her hair, as though needing to touch her and make certain she was real.

His touch felt very real and sent tingling waves of pleasure coursing through her body.

She glanced down at herself and noticed that she was clad only in a linen nightshirt. A man's nightshirt that was clearly too big for her and kept sliding off her shoulders. Bhrodi's, no doubt. But the impropriety of the situation paled in importance to the ordeal they'd just experienced. "How did I get here? Wherever *here* is. What happened? You were shot. Oh, and that serpent. I thought it was going to eat us." She gasped. "Lucinda's brother!"

His big, warm hand covered hers. "Dylan de Courcy is fine"

"He survived?"

Bhrodi nodded. "But his father didn't. Let me have one of my maids bring up some broth and light refreshments for you, and then we'll talk. There's much I need to say to you. But first, you need to recover your strength."

"I'm fine, Bhrodi. Truly. What time is it?" Her chamber was illuminated by candlelight, its luminescent glow appearing to make the light blue silk drapes and matching silk covers of her large, canopied bed shimmer like starlight. She glanced down at herself again, recognizing the significance of her wearing his nightclothes and wondering what had happened to her own wet garments. "Am I at Pembroke? Does my father know I'm safe?"

She gave him no time to answer before she began to ask more questions. "Has anyone looked at your injury? How bad is it? How were we saved?"

Bhrodi moved to sit on the bed beside her.

She ought to have said something, but didn't. She needed him close, needed to be in his comforting embrace. Propriety no longer mattered. Her reputation was in ruins just by being here, no matter how innocently she'd arrived. Besides, he looked too magnificent to resist. He always did. Particularly now.

The bedchamber he'd placed her in was grand in furnishings and size, but it still felt divinely intimate because she was alone in here with Bhrodi. The door was closed and the drapes drawn. There was a warming fire in the hearth and candles were lit beside her night table. The mattress was the most comfortable she'd ever slept in. Despite the grandeur of her surroundings, she knew this was not his ducal bedchamber. The room was too feminine.

But she was definitely at Pembroke Hall.

She liked that Bhrodi had brought her here and was now sitting beside her. He was dressed casually in a crisp, white shirt that was open at the collar and black trousers that molded to his finely formed legs. He wore polished black boots, but hadn't bothered to don a vest or cravat or jacket, for that matter. It struck her as odd that she could see no sign of bandages beneath his shirt. Nor did he appear to be weak or in pain. Had she not seen the streak of blood across his chest and known he was shot, she would never have believed he'd been injured.

Indeed, he looked splendid and powerful and dangerous.

His hair was dry and gleamed a magnificent ebony black. His eyes were gray, smoldering embers. His nicely formed lips twitched upward in a smile. "Any more questions?"

She laughed. "Lots, but I suppose I ought to allow you to answer the ones I've already asked. I don't understand how we're alive."

He reached out and caressed her cheek. "Because of you, Prudence. You're not only smart and beautiful, but you're one of the bravest persons I've ever met."

She gazed at him in confusion. "But I couldn't hold on to you. That last wave hit me as I tried to pull Dylan toward us. It pushed me hard against the wall. I never reached Dylan and I let go of you when I passed out."

"You held on to me long enough for me to recover my strength."

"And you saved Dylan? I'm glad." She had grown up with Dylan and Lucinda, and would never believe he had a nefarious bone in his body. Even at an age when brothers were supposed to be teasing and taunting their younger siblings, Dylan was always kind to Lucinda. That kindness had extended to her as well. "I'm truly grateful to you."

Bhrodi sighed and ran a hand roughly across the nape of his neck. "It wasn't me exactly, although I meant to save him. But not for any heroic purposes. I needed someone from that boat alive to name names and provide details."

Prudence's eyes widened as a wild thought struck her. "Are you suggesting that the serpent saved him?"

Bhrodi nodded. "For that reason, I've quietly confined Dylan to his home for the moment and not told anyone that he was on the boat. Death is the punishment for treason, and I know the Crown will sentence him to death if word gets out. So, if anyone asks… he was on the beach looking for his sister when he saw the boat approach us and ran to help."

So many feelings flooded Prudence all at once that it took her a moment to get her words out. Her throat was tight and scratchy when she finally did. "The serpent might have saved him in the water, but you're saving him now. I'm so thankful you believe in his innocence, but why are you doing this? I'm certain Dylan had no hand in this treachery because I've known him all my life. I expect that his father lured him onto the boat for the purpose of revealing his mad plan and having Dylan join him at his side to rule over a newly conquered Wales."

Bhrodi laughed mirthlessly. "That's exactly what Dylan said."

"Because it's the truth. But you don't know Dylan at all. Why have you spared him? Is it because your serpent spared him?" She took a deep breath and asked the question that frightened her most. "Are you… are you the serpent?"

He shifted uncomfortably, but his assessing, silver gaze never left her face. "I was raised on tales of my ancestor, the Serpent, and the rumored power he held over a mythical beast that protected his lands. The Serpent's blood runs in me, I can never deny it after all that has happened to us. For the first time in my life, I felt his power flow through my limbs and course through my blood. There is no doubt that the sea serpent and I are connected. But that creature is not an extension of me. I do not control it. Nor does it control me. We work together for the common goal of protecting Wales."

She frowned. "But I heard you summon it with your low growl."

"No, I was responding to its presence. Perhaps I was speaking to it and did not realize it. However, the serpent emerged from those watery depths and began to quietly circle that doomed boat long before we ever noticed its presence. I was not thinking of that creature until the moment it slithered across my chest. My only thought before and after it appeared, was to save you. Those men were traitors. They were traitors and they were coming to kill you. I couldn't allow that. I meant to fight them off by myself and keep fighting until I took my last breath. No one was going to touch you while I had an ounce of life left in me. But if I truly did control the sea serpent, then I am not sorry that I commanded it to kill anyone who threatened your life."

"And not yours?"

"I fight my own battles. I do not fear my own death." He reached out and caressed her cheek. "Pru, do you not realize yet what you mean to me?"

His voice was soft and throaty as he spoke the last, its deep, sensual rumble shooting tingles through her body. "No, Bhrodi. You've never told me how you felt, other than to chase me off your lands."

His grin simply melted her bones. "I'll have to remedy that, won't I?" He shifted his big body once more and leaned toward her. "I'm going to kiss you, Prudence. I'm going to kiss you as I've longed to kiss you since the first time I tried to toss you off my lands."

Oh, heavens! Yes, she wanted his kiss so much. "I want you to know that you're the only man I've ever kissed. And the only man I ever wish to kiss for the rest of my life."

"Are you proposing to me again, Prudence?"

She winced. "Did it sound like one? Have I just chased you away again because you don't wish to marry me? I know there is a difference between desiring a kiss, which is merely lust, and desiring my heart, which would mean you love me. So, are you going to kiss me because you lust for me – I'm quite flattered, by the way – or because you love me as much as I love you?"

He nudged her onto her back so that she rested against the elegant, soft pillows, and then he placed his hands on either side of her body to gently trap her. His body was now inches from hers. His lips were poised temptingly close to her lips.

His silver gaze held the smoldering promise of magic to come. "The answer ought to be obvious," he said in a husky whisper, closing his mouth over hers with what felt like lustful abandon. But as he deepened the kiss, deepening the pressure of his mouth against hers, it began to feel like something far more precious and everlasting.

She was in his embrace now, for his muscled arms had circled around her body and drawn her up against his hard chest at the same time he'd lowered his lips to hers. His kiss, the possessive crush of his mouth against hers, the embrace that held her captive in his arms, revealed he meant to claim her for his own. But how did one tell the difference between these powerful feelings of lust and love? How long would he want her to warm his bed? One night?

Or forever?

To her shame, she would accept whatever he offered. No, she wasn't ashamed of her feelings. It wasn't a matter of her being weak or helpless to resist his seductive advances, but a matter of remaining true to her heart.

She'd given her heart to him and could never give it to another.

She was his, whether he wanted her for one night or a good long while.

His tongue teased along the seam of her lips and gently forced them open to thrust inside in plundering conquest. His hands left a trail of heat wherever they roamed along her back, and when he slid one hand downward to catch the hem of her nightshirt and pull it up, her breath hitched. His palm felt warm and exciting against her bare skin as he eased the garment off her so that all of her was now shockingly bared to his view.

She'd never been like this with a man before, and yet she didn't feel afraid or in any way diminished to be subject to his gaze. "Bhrodi... I..."

"Let me look at you, Prudence. You're so beautiful." How many times had he spoken similar words to a woman in his bed? But there was something gentle and assuring in Bhrodi's expression that calmed her while at the same time arousing her. Her blood felt as though it was on fire. Her skin was suddenly intensely sensitive to his touch.

She tried to cover herself, hardly recognizing the wanton feelings he aroused in her with merely a steamy gaze. She did not know how to stop the throbbing heat now pulsing through her body and awakening sensations in her most intimate places. She did not know how to calm her rapidly beating heart or the fluttering in her belly.

"I want you, Prudence. I want you for my wife. I want you for always."

"You do?" She held her breath as she watched him slowly remove his shirt and toss it aside. She'd always thought him powerful, but he was so much more than that. He was muscle and sinew and taut strength. She reached out and slid her hand along the bulging muscles of his upper arms that were as solid as granite.

He arched an eyebrow and smiled wickedly, but allowed her to continue to explore him.

So, she did. She ran her fingers lightly along the

dark hairs on his chest, careful to avoid the stitches along his raw, red flesh where he'd been struck and almost killed. The shot had left an ugly gash, and would leave a noticeable scar when it healed.

But it would heal and that's all that mattered.

She traced her fingers downward to follow that trail of dark hair that disappeared below his taut stomach. There was nothing soft about this man except for the loving expression in his eyes. Was it possible he loved her? "A duke in love with the local magistrate's daughter," she murmured, speaking more to herself than to him.

"It happened often enough over the course of history."

"But this is you, and you're the powerful Duke of Pembroke. There is nothing to stop you from taking me now and offering me nothing in return."

His expression darkened. "Prudence, I will not take you unless I know you've consented to be my wife. Do you think so little of me that you think I would?"

"No, Bhrodi. I know you would never intentionally hurt me. The doubt lies within me. I haven't been raised to be a duchess. I'm a dotty bird lady," she tried to explain, for she knew he was a man of honor. This was her Bhrodi and he would never harm her in any way. "You're angry now."

"No, just disappointed. I love you, Prudence."

She smiled. "Say it again. Those words sounded very nice."

He kissed her softly on the mouth, drawing her up against the heat of his chest so that their bodies were pressed against each other, his muscle and her soft skin. His roughly stitched scar was a reminder of how close that shot had come to striking his heart. A little higher. A little deeper. He wouldn't be alive. The realization caused a wave of anguish to wash over her heart. "We were so fortunate, Bhrodi. How did we ever survive?"

"Because we had each other." He emitted a ragged groan. "I love you. I intend to marry you as soon as I obtain the special license. I'd do it today if I could, but I'll first need to obtain royal approval. I've already made the formal request, but I don't intend to wait more than another day for it."

"A day? But how is it possible to send a messenger there and back in that little time? And what if your request is denied?"

"It won't be."

"How can you be so certain? I'm just–"

"A magistrate's daughter?" Now he was scowling at her, obviously angrier than before. "Your stature is far higher than mine, if truth be told. The dukes of Pembroke have long been the protectors of Wales. But who do you think protects the dukes of Pembroke?"

"The serpent, of course."

"That serpent didn't pull me out of the water. That serpent didn't hold me in its arms and put the kiss of life in me." He shook his head and laughed lightly. "Thank goodness. I much preferred your kiss. You saved my life, Prudence. You saved Wales. The serpent and I had a small hand in it, but this mad plot was foiled because of you."

He stilled her when she meant to protest.

"And let me make one thing perfectly clear. I'm not offering to marry you out of a sense of obligation. I want to marry you because I cannot imagine my life without you by my side. Not as my protector, although you certainly are that. But as my wife. As the woman I love and want to hold in my arms for the full course of our lives. Share my life with me, Prudence. Share my bed. Share my happiness, for there will not be a sad day for me while you are beside me."

She closed her eyes to take in the import of his words, smiling because these were so much better than the stern ones he'd issued when chasing her off his land. Of course, he'd done it because he'd wanted to keep her and the members of the Pembroke chapter of the Ladies Birdwatching Society safe, but she hadn't known it at the time. "Bhrodi, I'd be honored. Yes, my love. Although I must point out that I asked you first. In truth, it is you who owes me an answer."

He kicked off his boots and stretched out on the bed beside her, placing one arm under her to tuck her to his side. "To be precise," he said, rolling slightly toward her so that he leaned over her, the weight of him so splendid against her body, "you asked me to reconsider your proposal. I have reconsidered it."

His kiss was long and lingering and deliciously possessive. "I am accepting it. We're bound to each other now, Prudence."

She circled her arms around his neck and smiled. "Then you'll be my husband?"

"Yes, my heart is forever yours."

He gave her no chance to say more before he moved his body over hers and dipped his head to kiss her. His hands roamed along her curves, touching her in places that were only a husband's right to claim. As he slid his hand along the swell of her breast, she felt the calloused pads of his fingers and the cuts that were still healing along his palm. But the roughness only served to enhance her building passion, for he was exquisitely gentle despite his own coiled need.

He touched her and took possession of her, and cupped his hand between her thighs to slide his fingers along her most intimate spot to prepare her for their coupling. She wanted this and wanted him, and was greedy to experience all that was special between two people who loved each other. She was ready when he entered her and filled her. She allowed the pulsing sensations to take free rein over her body and her soul.

She dug her fingers into his massive shoulders and held on as they rode to soaring heights, his movements as majestic as that of the golden hawks who flew among the coastal cliffs, his thrusts powerful and intimate and protective.

Their bodies moved as one, his damp skin now rubbing against the sensitive tips of her breasts, and then his mouth closed over one sensitive tip and he began to suckle and tease until she couldn't bear the pleasure of it and moaned. "Oh, Bhrodi. Oh… oh…"

The exquisite sensations built as they moved with each other, his thrusts slower and deeper and harder, until they were both rocked by the explosive force of their passion. Prudence cried out as she felt herself shatter into a million pieces of starlight. She wrapped her arms tightly around Bhrodi's hot, damp neck and kissed him as he spent himself inside of her, his liquid heat spilling deep, and traces of it spilling against her thighs as he slowly withdrew.

But he did not release her. Instead, he rolled her atop him and held her protectively and lovingly in his arms. "Prudence, my love. How do you feel?"

Her lips were full and swollen as she cracked a smile and rested her head against his chest. She felt the prickle of his stitches against her cheek and realized she should not be pressing down on them, although he did not seem to mind. She nestled in the crook of his shoulder instead. "I feel like a duchess who is very much loved."

He laughed softly. "I never meant to take my desire for you that far. I meant to show you pleasure, but take none for myself until you were properly my wife. I had better obtain the special license first thing in the morning."

Her heart was racing. Although she felt completely safe in Bhrodi's arms, there was no doubt that there was a majestic wildness to this duke that would make all their couplings a delicious adventure. She liked that Bhrodi was as wild and untamed as the wind along the ocean cliffs. As wild as a storm-tossed sea.

As wild as the serpent of legend.

She'd fallen in love with Bhrodi for all that he was.

He ran his hands lightly up and down her arms as he cradled her in his embrace. "Your father has already given his consent. I obtained it the day the serpent destroyed Emrys de Courcy's boat."

She glanced up at him in confusion. "You mean to say that you obtained it today? When did you have the time?"

"Today? No, Prudence. That day was three days ago. You've been drifting in and out of consciousness ever since."

The blood drained from her face and her heart gave a little lurch. "Three days? Are you serious?"

He turned on his side to face her, his brow furrowed. "Quite serious. I was mad with worry. I haven't left your side these past two days. Had I realized how badly you were injured, I would never have left you that first day either, not even for a moment. But there was too much to do, and you were so brave throughout the ordeal, I never thought that you would be in danger."

He propped up on one elbow and continued. "We summoned the local doctor to tend to my wounds and treat your concussion. I left you in the capable hands of my staff while I went into town with Bigbury and Colliers. We had Dylan de Courcy in our custody, of course."

She nodded and hugged herself to him while he continued, for she needed to feel the heat of him against her. She needed to breath him in and burrow herself against the hard strength of his body. She closed her eyes and listened to his deep, comforting voice. "While Bigbury questioned him, Colliers conducted a search of his home. Colliers then went to inform your father and the town council about what had happened."

"Did he tell them about the sea serpent?"

"Yes, there was no getting around it. The bodies of the traitors began to wash upon the shore." He sighed and gently ran his hands through her hair. "As soon as we're married, I must return to London to report to the

Crown and Parliament. This plot we foiled today is no small matter. Dylan was very helpful. So were Lucinda's sketch books which were untouched in her bedchamber when we searched."

Prudence gasped. How could she have forgotten about her best friend? "But what of Lucinda? Have you found her?"

He chuckled. "Rest easy, my love. She eloped with the local blacksmith, Charles Frayne. They'd planned to run off as soon as the town council meeting disbanded, and that's just what they did. She had no idea what her father had planned, and her disappearance was mere coincidence."

Prudence closed her eyes and swallowed hard. "Thank goodness. I knew she and Dylan could not have been a part of their father's madness."

His mirth also seemed to fade away. He kissed the top of her head and then continued to gently run his fingers through her hair. "I suppose it can be said that love saved Lucinda. I don't think she would have been spared had she been spotted at Llangolyn Rock studying your birds. Her father was completely mad. He would have destroyed anyone who got in his way, perhaps even his own beloved daughter."

She hugged Bhrodi. "I'm so glad it's over. It is over, isn't it?"

"I think so. Bigbury and Colliers are following all the clues that Dylan gave them. There are other traitors left to be captured, but none from around here. Any local conspirators have all been safely rounded up and imprisoned."

"What a mad, hopeless scheme. Whatever put the idea in Emrys de Courcy's head? Madness takes many paths. Why did he choose this particular one?"

"His mother – Dylan and Lucinda's grandmother – was a descendant of the Wynn family, and she probably instilled this madness in him at an early age. They are one of the few families who can claim blood ties to the old Welsh kings."

"Ah, greed and the lust for power were his motives."

"Prudence, I almost lost you because of his madness." His voice was soft and ragged with deeply felt relief. "I never want us to be apart again. But I must go to London. I'd like you to go with me as my duchess. I know I'm asking much of you, so I will understand if you'd rather not."

"I would go to the ends of the earth with you, my

love." She grinned as she trailed her hand down his chest and lower, for he had removed his trousers before they'd coupled, so they were both without their clothes and she was no longer shy about exploring his body as thoroughly as he'd explored hers. "I'm sure there are fascinating birds to study wherever you shall take me."

He threw his head back and laughed. "That's my Prudence. I'm glad you're back, my love."

"It will take more than a wicked Mongoose to best a dotty bird lady."

"That name will never do for you, my love. From this day forward, you shall be known as the Fiery Maiden of Mor."

She laughed heartily. "Ah, I'm to be a fiery maiden of the sea? I think the townspeople of Pembroke will find it as ridiculous as I do. Fiery, indeed. What silliness."

"Very well, what shall I call you then?"

"Prudence will do. Or *my duchess* will do nicely as well. *My love* will do best of all."

"Very well… my love."

"Good, that's settled." She rubbed her body invitingly against his. "Bhrodi, are you tired?"

"Not in the least." He kissed her softly on the mouth, understanding what she was asking.

"I'm not either."

Grinning wickedly, he took her into his arms and rolled her under him. "We'll have to think of something to do then. I know just the thing."

"I'm sure you do." Prudence wasn't experienced enough to take the lead. Bhrodi knew what he was doing. Indeed, as his big body settled over her, and his hands explored her intimately, and his lips and the soft, flicks of his teasing tongue stirred her to heightened passions, she had never had more fun in an evening.

The hot sensations and decadent moans he evoked from her...oh, heavens. She had no idea that coupling could be so exquisitely enjoyable.

Perhaps she was a fiery maiden, after all.

CHAPTER NINE

Three Months Later

BHRODI SMILED AS he watched Prudence scamper off Llangolyn Rock and make her way toward him. Sundown approached early in December and the golden ball in the sky had already begun to sink low on the horizon, leaving behind a brilliant tapestry of pinks, burnt oranges, and purple streaks across the sky. The white, tufted clouds appeared to be glowing as the sun's rays shone behind them, and the tranquil sea glistened as though pearls had been cast across the vast expanse.

Bhrodi loved the sea and land, but he loved nothing better than Prudence. Indeed, he'd never tire of looking at this beautiful woman who'd conquered his heart the moment he'd first seen her standing on that outcropping, her flaming hair billowing against the wind and her magnificent body outlined against the fabric of her gown. "Any discoveries today, my love?"

"A few. Hamlet and Ophelia are now a matched pair. Come, have a look. They've built their nest where Romeo and Juliet had theirs." She turned to gaze across the outcropping toward the cliff walls and the caves below, her expression momentarily wistful. "I hope they'll have a happy life."

Bhrodi moved to stand behind her, drawing her into his arms so that she was now swallowed in his cloak to keep her warm while they both looked out across the cliffs and icy sea. Her back was pressed against his chest and her head rested against his shoulder. "You have to stop naming them as doomed lovers," he teased. "How about naming them after a couple who managed to find their happily ever after?"

"Such as Bhrodi and Prudence?" She turned to face him, still buried in his cloak. Grinning, she reached up on her toes to kiss him.

"They would be a happy couple, indeed," he said, meaning every word. He'd spent almost thirty years on his own and a mere three months married to Prudence, but he had already amassed more happy memories during their marriage than he'd had in his life before they'd met. He was the proud Serpent. He wasn't the sentimental sort, and would never be, except when it came to Prudence.

She threw her arms around him and kissed him again. "The sun's going down. It will be dark soon."

He arched an eyebrow. "What are you suggesting?"

"Must I say it?" She was still grinning at him like a kitten who had just licked her fill of sweet cream. "Or would you rather I occupy myself elsewhere. I could call a meeting of the Ladies Birdwatching Society, and–"

He gave a mock shudder. "Perish the thought. I find that I am suddenly fatigued and would like nothing better than to retire early. Care to join me, Duchess Pru?"

"I'd love nothing better, Your Grace."

He swept her into his arms.

She gave a little cry and swatted his shoulder. "What are you doing? I can walk."

"I know. But I think this is how you fell in love with me. You'd twisted your ankle and I came to your rescue. You lost your heart to me when I caught you up in my muscled and manly arms."

She laughed heartily in response to his wicked grin. "You've long since won that battle, Bhrodi de Shera. You know I'm wildly in love with you." But in the next moment, she cleared her throat and turned disquiet-ingly serious. "There seems to be no point in waiting, now that you do have me in your arms."

He stopped walking and stared at her, his humor fading as hers had. "In waiting for what, Pru?"

"Your Yuletide gift, of course. I was going to tell you after the celebration we're hosting for the town tomorrow, but this feels so right and I can no longer contain myself."

He eased when her smile returned, but he was still confused. "You didn't need to get me a gift, my love."

"Oh, but I had no choice in the matter. This little gift was most persistent." She kissed him tenderly on the cheek. "We're going to have a baby, my love. I'm three months along."

"Pru…" Her words left him speechless. A cool breeze swirled around them, but he felt nothing but warmth. Then suddenly, a glint in the coastal waters caught his eye. He turned toward it and saw the elongated body of the sea serpent that had saved him and Prudence those same three months ago.

Prudence inhaled lightly. "Bhrodi, look. Do you see him?"

He nodded. "I do."

"Do you think he knows we're to have a child?"

"Yes, my love. I think this is his way of giving his blessing." But he held Prudence a little tighter, for he'd almost lost her that day and his heart still hadn't fully recovered. They watched in silence as its glistening body made several passes in the cove and then disappeared from view.

"Where has he gone?" she asked.

Bhrodi's gaze swept across the white caps that had formed upon the wave crests. "Back to his cave, I imagine. We won't see him again unless there is another threat to Wales."

She lovingly stroked his cheek. "Or a threat to you, the valiant protector of Wales."

The chill wind gusted and the sun sank lower upon the horizon. "Come, my love. This valiant protector is eager to get his hands all over you. Gently, of course. Now that you're with child. Our child. Pru, you may be carrying the next Duke of Pembroke...the next legendary Serpent."

She smiled impishly and tugged lightly on his hair. "Or the next chairwoman of the Pembroke chapter of the Ladies Birdwatching Society."

He shook his head and gave a laughing groan.

"That would be wonderful, too."

He continued to walk back to Pembroke Hall with Prudence in his arms, his thoughts now in a whirl. He would be a father soon. Would he be a good one? Pru was now smiling broadly and he knew her heart was overflowing with happiness.

"You will be the best father any child could have," she said, seeming to read his thoughts. His concern must have been obvious. "You're the Serpent. I know you'll protect our children as fiercely as you protect Wales."

He nodded, knowing so would she. The realization calmed him. Indeed, he knew their children would always be loved and protected, not only by him, but by Prudence.

They entered the house and he carried her upstairs to their bedchamber. He still wanted to put his hands all over his beautiful wife, but knew he had to be gentle. Perhaps he had better not touch her.

Apparently, Pru did not agree. "Make love to me, Bhrodi."

So he did, but slowly and sweetly, and when they were spent and he'd wrapped her in his arms, he gave her a long, lingering kiss. "I love you, Prudence

Pertwee de Shera. I shall love you and our children always. I give you my word of honor."

She rested her chin on his chest and grinned up at him impudently. "And I give you the same oath. For you may be the protector of Wales, but I am your protector and will always be. I suppose you could say I am your Serpentess."

He caressed her cheek. "There is no such word. Anyway, you're far too beautiful to be a serpent."

"Then what am I?"

"I should think it would be obvious. You watched over me. You saved me. You're my angel."

She gave it a moment's consideration and then nodded. "Bhrodi's angel. Yes, I think I like the sound of that."

THE END

ALSO BY MEARA PLATT

FARTHINGALE SERIES
My Fair Lily
The Duke I'm Going To Marry
Rules For Reforming A Rake
A Midsummer's Kiss
The Viscount's Rose
Capturing The Heart Of A Cameron

KINDLE WORLD SERIES
Nobody's Angel
Kiss An Angel
Bhrodi's Angel

DARK GARDENS SERIES
Garden of Shadows
Garden of Light
Garden of Dragons
Garden of Destiny

THE BRAYDENS
A Match Made In Duty
Earl of Westcliff

My Dear Readers,

Thank you for giving *Bhrodi's Angel* a read. If you enjoyed it, then please consider leaving a review – it is most appreciated! I chose to write in the world of The Serpent because I love that Kathryn Le Veque's hero is the mythical protector of Wales. So I made up my Regency hero, Bhrodi de Shera, the Duke of Pembroke, who is a descendant of the Serpent, and the current protector of Wales. In my story, Bhrodi de Shera meets his match in Prudence Pertwee, the magistrate's daughter who steals his heart. While Bhrodi is known as the Serpent, he finds that there is more to the myth than even he realized, for there is a real serpent who swims within the waters off the coast of Pembroke, and they share a connection. The medieval Bhrodi de Shera is another of Kathryn Le Veque's wonderful heroes. Her Serpent faced the very real threat of English conquest of Wales. In Kathryn's story, the Serpent is matched with the youngest daughter of the legendary William de Wolfe. I hope Prudence, my Regency heroine, makes her proud. She's smart and brave, and not afraid to fight for her convictions.

Writing is a joy for me, and to be able to participate in Kathryn Le Veque's de Wolfe Pack World is a thrill. *Bhrodi's Angel* is my third story in this de Wolfe Pack World. If you enjoyed it, I hope you'll give *Nobody's Angel* and *Kiss An Angel* a try. They are the other two Regency novellas I've written for her world and those stories are based on one of Kathryn's most popular de Wolfe series books, *Lion Of The North*. I dare you not to fall in love with Titus de Wolfe!

What makes Kathryn's stories so memorable is the heart and courage of the proud warriors she creates and the women who are worthy to stand as equals by their side. If you have a little time for more lighthearted Regency romances, I invite you to Chipping Way, one of the prettiest streets in London's Mayfair district, to meet my bestselling Farthingale sisters, Lily, Daffodil, Daisy, Laurel, and Rose Farthingale as they manage to find love amid the chaos of their respective debut seasons. Laurel's story, *A Midsummer's Kiss*, is the 2017 RONE award winner for best Regency. If you prefer your historical romances with a paranormal flair, then I would love you to try my Dark Gardens series and meet the Fae warriors and dragonshifters who find love with their very worthy, mortal heroines. Please visit my website: www.mearaplatt.com and subscribe to my newsletter for a gift Farthingale novella from me. You'll also learn of special events, prizes, contests and much more from me and other historical romance authors.

Cheers!

Meara

About the Author

Meara Platt is a USA Today bestselling author and an award winning Amazon UK All-star. She has traveled the world, occasionally lectures, and always finds time to write. Her favorite place in all the world is England's Lake District, which may not come as a surprise since many of her stories are set in that idyllic landscape, including her Romance Writers of America Golden Heart award winning story now titled Garden of Dragons which is Book 3 in her paranormal romance Dark Gardens series. Her lighthearted Farthingale series story, A Midsummer's Kiss, is the 2017 RONE award winner for best Regency. Learn more about Meara Platt by visiting her website at www.mearaplatt.com.

CPSIA information can be obtained
at www.ICGtesting.com
Printed in the USA
LVHW080545110319
610184LV00014B/218/P